HIGH SPIRITS

J. T. CROFT

FLAME TREE PRESS

First published by Elmfire Press 2020

Copyright ©2020 by J. T. Croft

First edition

ISBN 978-1-8381089-1-5

Elmfire Press

Unit 35590,

PO Box 15113,

Birmingham, B2 2NJ

United Kingdom

www.jtcroft.com

ACKNOWLEDGMENTS

For all those spirits who continue to interfere for the good in everyone's lives.

To my parents who have always loved and supported me. No book on parenting could have prepared you for my eccentricities.
(I'm sorry for pulling the fish tank over, aged six.)

To Tracey, for putting up with my non-author alter-ego.

CONTENTS

THE SPIRIT OF THE PLACE

'*Don't forget the beans,*' it said.

'Anything else?' Agnes replied, squinting down at the little pad of paper only inches from her cataract-glazed eyes.

'*You're low on toilet rolls, too,*' replied the voice, coming from inside the pantry.

'Much obliged to you as always,' said Agnes, shutting the door. 'My memory is getting worse.'

'*You must get a plaster ready,*' said the voice, now present in the kitchen. '*You will cut your finger later on.*'

Agnes shuffled to the downstairs loo and looked into the mirror.

'Oh drat. Will I be all right?' she said.

She stared at her reflection, gentle and time-worn, waiting for the reply.

'*Nothing to worry about, but just get it ready,*' said the voice.

Agnes's shaking hands fumbled with the box of plasters on the narrow shelf of the bathroom cupboard. She feared cutting herself but dreaded the foreknowledge that she would cut herself. It was always such an effort with her arthritic fingers struggling to open and peel back the plastic covering of the sticky protective bandages.

The rows of medicine bottles and pillboxes were overwhelming. Agnes couldn't recall what ailment most of them were supposed to ease. She pointed at a sugar-encrusted top belonging to a tall, thin blue-glass bottle.

'That looks old. Whatever that is, do I need to buy any more?' she asked, worrying that she hadn't used it in a while.

'*No, that's for your constipation,*' said the voice. '*You take the brown pill for that now.*'

'Did I swallow one this morning?' Agnes asked.

The voice was reassuring. '*Yes, you also took the blue and the pink tablets, before you ask.*'

She looked at her crooked and thickened fingers that had once been so soft and supple.

'I used to have lovely nails,' she said, to the empty room.

'*And lustrous hair,*' the voice replied. '*Do you remember the time when the greengrocer asked you for a lock of it?*'

Agnes's dry and cracked lips broke into a broad grin. 'It was a spring day...'

'*It was in August.*'

'Stop interrupting,' she said. 'I only went in for a pound of tomatoes, and I came out with my lipstick smudged and an offer to the dance.'

She shuffled, youthful with the memory, to the hallway to pick up her purse.

'*I liked him, but he only called once.*'

'What do you expect?' Agnes replied. 'Talking to thin air put him off.'

'*Don't forget your scarf,*' said the voice, ignoring the suggestion that Agnes was a spinster because of its presence. '*It's cold outside the post office, and you will need to queue. Miss Pugh will be late again.*'

Agnes continued to think of the dark and handsome grocer with the Brylcreem-groomed hair.

'I can't even remember his name now, but I know I outlived him and the rest of them. Except for that barber over at Bisley; I haven't seen him in twenty years.'

She struggled into a camel-coloured coat and picked up her keys. The tartan trolley bag was waiting on the porch, ready to be let out, like a dog desperate for its constitutional walk to the shops.

'*You will outlive them all, my dear, even him,*' came the reply. '*I'd think about getting a new hat, though.*'

'What's wrong with the one I'm wearing?' she asked, wheeling the squeaking trolley bag outside and alerting the nosey net-curtain twitchers across the street of her imminent departure.

'*He's going to pass away in a few weeks, and the funeral will be two months this Thursday. I only mention it because there is a sale on at the moment at Marks and Spencer. You could go to town this afternoon.*'

'What time is the bus?'

There was a moment's reflection as the voice retired to consider the question. Agnes looked back through the roundel-paned window of the door. The barber had been the last living person ever to kiss her. Nobody would recall her luscious red lips and the coiffed beehive in a few weeks.

'*There's a bus at 2.17 pm and another at 2.57 pm, but that one drops you off at Talbot Street, and you'll need to walk further,*' said the voice, mimicking the style of a ticket inspector.

She dragged the wooden door across the threadbare mat, leaving a crack to whisper through.

'I won't be long, my dear,' she said, continuing the tradition of over sixty years.

'*Don't be,*' it said. '*There's a Stewart Granger film on at one o'clock, and it'll take your mind off the letter that will arrive while you are out.'*

'*Moonfleet?*' she asked.

'*No,*' it replied. '*The other one.*'

She pulled the door shut several times to engage the worn lock.

———

SHE ALWAYS FELT A PANG OF GUILT, LEAVING IT ALONE BY itself when she went out. Agnes had asked on countless occasions whether it would like to come out, but it had consistently declined, content to stay in the house, or unable to leave it. It never complained about being on its own, and Agnes was glad of the company when she returned. Ever since her dog had died, the only regular contact had been with the postman, the woman at the supermarket cigarette counter, and the infrequent home help. The telephone line was no longer needed when everyone in her address book was now six feet under at the local churchyard. She missed the occasional cold callers and their sales pitches. Slowly and surely they removed her from the lists that percolated amongst the companies; there weren't any leads generated, and the twenty-minute chats were costing them money.

She also missed going through the obituaries in the local newspaper. She had looked forward to the ritual of crossing off the names with a sad shake of the head before she ploughed into the word-search next to it.

Agnes buttoned her coat and put on her threadbare mink gloves. She tottered to the end of the overgrown path, listing side to side like a Spanish galleon in a rough sea. The trolley bag banged and bumped its empty way over the uneven crazy paving, joyful to be along for the road trip.

'Is she talking to herself again?' asked the neighbour across the street, finishing his breakfast.

His nosey wife watched as Agnes dismounted the steps to the pavement with all the grace of an eighty-year-old rheumatic mountain goat.

'Yes, at the door a moment ago,' she replied. 'Poor thing. It must be lonely when nobody answers you back.' She turned around to her husband reading the paper, oblivious to her last comment, and the next.

'I know just how she feels.'

THE BRIEF WALK INTO THE VILLAGE YIELDED THREE 'GOOD mornings' on the way to the post office. A queue had formed outside the locked door and provided an excellent opportunity to discuss the weather with the expectant mother in front. It was chilly for April, and she was glad of the scarf now that the voice's prediction had come true. It always did, and the most trivial protection afforded by the voice's divination comforted her most of the time.

She had tried to game the system decades before by asking it for the lottery numbers. It was useless at that, or deliberately so. *'Winning that will be the death of you,'* it had said, after much insistence. *'I'll make sure you don't run out of money.'* She had loved filling in the football pools, but it took no interest if Bournemouth versus Sheffield Wednesday would end up being a score draw. So she stopped asking the voice for tips and won little for the following ten years, along with everyone else.

It provided most remarkably and thoughtfully. It would predict the location and owner of a dropped wallet or a golden ring. Often the person was so pleased to get the item back that a reward of more than a few pounds made its way into Agnes's hands, despite her protestations. It was only later, waking in the middle of the night, that they wondered how she had known where to find them.

On those days, she would buy sausages or lamb chops from the expensive butchers in the high street. She would also bring home flowers, much to the delight of the voice.

The postwoman bustled red-faced and menopausal into view before unlocking the door to the post office and bursting into tears. The customers filed in and helped her into the back room until the distraught shopkeeper could slide up the counter screen. She began selling stamps and issuing pension payments, in between snivels and the blowing of her long nose.

Agnes bought a lottery ticket.

'Jackpot tonight, Agnes,' said the tear-streaked post-woman, and the only one to use her name with any regularity. 'Something tells me you'll be on a yacht in the Bahamas this time next week.'

Agnes grinned back. 'Do you have a spirit around the place too?'

The woman's eyes brimmed with woe. 'I wish I did,' she said, bursting into fresh waves of tears. 'I don't even have a boyfriend anymore; he's left me for that harlot from number twenty-three.'

Agnes tried to comfort her through the screen. A few queuing villagers, eager for gossip, crowded around and offered their sympathies and their telephone numbers, just in case the poor woman felt like spilling the whole sordid incident exclusively to them later. Agnes squeezed back through the scrum and made her way to the small convenience store, to be served by the victorious glamour-puss from number twenty-three. She ambled home via the park to feed the pigeons.

These days, her creaking joints were even gladder to see

the terraced alms-house that she had lived in for seventy years. She remembered seeing it as a child, when she'd moved from the busy town of Stroud to the new village idyll. The terrace had been recently converted from an old shell-shock hospital; the nurses had gone, and the young families had moved in. It was the first time she had ever had a garden to play in, and she now had a bedroom to herself. Her parents had loved the place, right up until they had died within a year of each other. They had left her, at eighteen years old, with a sizeable mortgage and an enormous problem.

The voice had appeared shortly after, and not out loud at first, but distant and fuzzy like an imaginary friend. She had welcomed the sound of it in the empty house despite the doctor's diagnosis that it was a result of grief-induced shock. The doctors refused to listen to her assurances that the imaginary friend was real and looking after her, so she stopped going to see them and gave into its warm and comforting protection. It was sharp with noticing medical problems ahead of time and always had the right prognosis. It was also great at finishing the crossword when she got stuck.

She shoved open the door. 'Only me, my dear.'

'*The letter from social services is in the letterbox,*' the voice replied. '*They are coming on Friday morning to assess you.*'

Agnes took off her coat and pulled the envelope through the plastic-bristled letterbox. 'The postwoman lost her fella, my dear.'

'*Yes, but she will meet someone special the week after next. He'll propose to her in September.*'

Agnes opened the leather tongue of the tattered tartan trolley and emptied the contents onto the kitchen table slowly and stiffly.

'*Would you like me to read the letter to you?*' asked the voice. '*It's important, and I want to know you'll be all right about it.*'

'They think I need putting in a home, but I've got one

here, and I've got you,' she said, ignoring the offer of help. 'It's not time for me to go yet, is it?'

Agnes put the kettle on, then got out the knife to cut the carrots for lunch. Her hands shook more than ever, and the thought of the people trying to take away her independence was making things worse. She grabbed the carrot and aimed the blade downwards.

She only bled for a few minutes before she remembered where the ready-and-waiting plaster was.

'*Are you all right, my dear?*' asked the voice, seeming sadder than usual.

'Blasted hands – can't grip, can't open the bleeding jars and can't cut carrots either,' Agnes replied.

The voice became calmer. '*Why don't you put the oven on then go have a nice sit-down. That nice young weatherman will be on before the film starts.*'

Agnes nodded and staggered back to the kitchen, leaving a thin one-handed streak of blood on the wall as she steadied herself. 'I'm getting so tired,' she said, before catching her breath. 'You won't let them take me away, will you? Not from here, and away from you?'

The voice quivered. It was usually so passive, and so sure.

'*You leave it to me and stop worrying about it. I know what's best for you, don't I? Get the spuds on; you won't hurt yourself any more today.*'

THE FOLLOWING MORNING, AGNES HAD DIFFICULTY getting out of bed. Her legs seemed cold and unresponsive, and she struggled to reach them and rub them back into life. There was a small pool of crimson on the sheets from the cut on her finger; her thinned warfarin-infused blood barely clotted anymore. She sat up, swinging her varicose legs to the floor, and waited for them to respond.

Agnes couldn't remember if she was getting up or going to bed, and the confusion lasted for several minutes. Light peeped through the faded curtains.

'Is it morning or evening, my dear?' she asked.

'*Morning, and you need to put your emergency response button around your neck,*' said the voice. '*You will have a little tumble later.*'

Agnes shrugged and reached with shaking hands to the bedside table, knocking over the clicking alarm clock. She stood and rocked precariously on her way to the bathroom. The voice was always discreet and would never discuss business during her ablutions. It had enjoyed the earliest years of their relationship in this very room, discussing many saucy things as the young and bubbly Agnes Brown had bathed ahead of her unsuccessful attempts at attracting the opposite sex. Now, it looked down in stricken sadness, like an owner knowing that a trip to the vets with some rapidly ailing pet was only a short time away.

The old woman had cured its loneliness for seventy years, and the approaching goodbye would be terrible.

I know what's best for you...

Her fall from the third tread of the carpeted stair happened an hour later, and the voice comforted her while the ambulance men broke in through the front door and lifted Agnes onto a trolley and away to the hospital for several days.

It had rarely known such silence, even when Agnes had taken up the courage to go away on holiday for a week to Weston-super-Mare. She had sent back postcards addressed to 'My Dear'. It knew Agnes would return, but not for long now. She would outlive the barber in Bisley, but not by much. The most painful part was not being able ever to hold her, or grasp the living flesh as it had once done amongst those poor boys from Flanders. It remembered being there for them, caring for the sick and the dying until it had succumbed one day to Spanish flu, in a bed right on this spot.

The spirit had always liked this part of the building and had stayed.

They wheeled Agnes back after three days, black and blue with bruises. The care workers moved the bed downstairs before the assessment later that day. A vacancy might arise at the rest home shortly, now that any obvious and life-threatening danger had passed. The workers noted the blood on the walls, the stain on the mattress, and the bedroom in disarray. They whispered and made notes.

'I'm back, my dear,' she said, without fear of being overheard.

It whispered in reply, in delight at seeing her. The support workers awkwardly smiled as Agnes continued. 'They can't sink old Agnes Brown, can they?' she said to the Artex ceiling.

The carers made Agnes comfortable and sat her down to watch *Celebrity Dominoes* on the tiny TV until the social care officer arrived to examine the reports. The carers retired to the dirty kitchen to discuss the procedure and the way forwards.

'*Agnes, my dear,*' the spirit said. '*Trust me now and do what I tell you.*'

'When have you ever let me down? They want to take me away, and it's not time yet, is it? You told me you'd look out for me, all those years ago now,' she replied.

'*I want you to take out both your hearing aids and put them on the coffee table.*'

'But I won't be able to hear what she's saying,' said Agnes.

'*You won't need to, my dear,*' it said. '*It will make you look younger and less... infirm. I'll be telling you what to say; I have experience in these matters.'*

Agnes thought about it before taking them out.

'They are coming back in five minutes,' the spirit lied. *'Are you ready? Why don't you tell me a few things you've enjoyed most about having me around?'*

Agnes began speaking, and the care team entered without warning.

'Well, my dear,' she said, oblivious that the assessment had started, 'there was that time you told me I would hate going blonde and my word when I looked in the mirror I was in a right state.'

The spirit recalled the incident tenderly and with a stab of grief as its betrayal played out.

'Hello, Agnes,' said the care officer, kneeling with a clipboard. 'Would it be all right to have a little chat?'

Agnes saw the woman's mouth move silently and heard the spirit's voice.

'Tell her, "Only if Alexa says it's okay."'

Agnes repeated the phrase, and looked up at the ceiling. 'Is Alexa your actual name, then? I never thought to ask in all these years!'

The officer looked confused. 'No, my name is Jane. Do you have an Alexa voice assistant in the room?'

'Oh yes,' said Agnes, managing to lip-read the last question, 'but she'll be cross I'm interrupting her, so let's be quiet now until she speaks again.'

The officer got up and called out to a non-existent digital assistant, 'Alexa, what is the time?'

There was silence.

'Not time to go yet, is it?' Agnes mouthed, repeating the instructions from the voice. The care worker looked down, noticing the hearing aids.

'Would you like to put these in, Agnes?' she asked.

'No, thank you. I'm fine. The spirit of the place says I look younger without them in.'

'Is the spirit of the place talking to you now, Agnes?'

'Yes, and I'm delighted to be here talking to myself all day. No need to worry about me. I will have a slip on the carpet tomorrow in a strange place, but the spirit says I'll be fine.'

'Thank you, Agnes,' said the officer. 'Would it be okay if you came to stay with me for a few days, just until we get this lovely house of yours tidied up?'

'Pleasure was all mine. Come again,' Agnes replied, oblivious to the sound of the death knell, tolling for the end of her independence.

The pain that the spirit thought it would feel was nothing like the reality of finally losing Agnes. The betrayal and break of trust was devastating, and it sobbed, almost to within hearing of the departing ambulance driver. Agnes flailed wildly in confusion, as she was being pushed into the transport, taking her away to her last home for the remaining few months.

It was all too much.

The spirit rushed at every window, to see the last glimpse of seventy years of companionship wheeled up the ramp, and into the care of others.

———

LATER THAT WEEK, RUDE MEN WITH NO REGARD FOR Agnes's things cleared the house which then lay unoccupied for months. Many people came to look around the empty, but not entirely soulless, interior, and a young family bought it at a discount and moved in. A little girl with her teddy bear in tow sat crying in the corner of the spare room. The move had taken her far away from her best friend and the school she had loved. The spirit folded her invisible arms around the child, and she stopped sobbing.

'*My dear,*' the voice whispered, '*tell me all about it.*'

The child looked up, surprised, and then at its bear. 'I'm all alone,' she said, staring into the black-button eyes.

'*So am I now,*' the spirit replied. '*I miss someone, too.*'

'What's your name?' asked the child.

'*You can call me... Agnes, my dear.*'

'I like that name. I'm Charlotte. Do you want to be my friend?'

'*Very much. I'll take good care of you. Would you like to help write a letter to my old friend?*'

AGNES LOOKED OUT DREAMILY FROM THE DAYROOM window, enjoying the view of the garden through the haze of the morphine. A slip on the carpet had fractured her hip, and she would never walk again in the few days she had left.

'Got a letter for you, Agnes, how unusual,' said the carer, coming in to check on her. 'Shall I read it to you?'

Agnes made a sign, and the carer put the folded paper into her lap. She looked down and opened it with shaking hands.

'There now,' said the carer. 'Look what that lovely little girl downstairs has drawn for you.'

On one side of the sheet was a bright scene scrawled in many colours of crayon. It showed a large bath and a dark-haired bee-hived woman, beaming, with bubbles and bright red lipstick. The caring image of a nurse in an old-fashioned uniform looked on, ghostly, from above.

The carer turned it over to read the single letters carefully drawn to be as legible as possible from one so young:

'*My dear, I'm sorry I did not say goodbye. You must forgive me for trying to look after you until the end. Do you know that you will go to sleep on Thursday, and when you wake up, you'll be able to see me? I'm looking forward to it so very much, and so is the greengrocer with the Brylcreem-groomed hair. He's playing cards with Stewart Granger at the moment and telling him of the time you came into the empty shop for a pound of tomatoes.*'

TYBURN'S SHADOW

Tom stood up in his stirrups and caught the first stench of eighteenth-century London. It was not an improvement from the acrid smoulder of autumn bonfires across the fields of Middlesex. The muddy miles had been a perpetual reminder of the disastrous fire, a burning so fierce that it had snuffed out the life of his dear father, their peaceful country smallholding, and his future. The following week dealing with the charred aftermath had been horrific.

It was a bright, chilly afternoon and the ordinary day's ride from St Albans to the city had been uneventful. Usually, the route was a pleasant experience but not on this occasion; he had a desperate cause in the capital. By tomorrow, the solicitor would have settled Tom's inheritance, and he would be returning home to rebuild the small manor house and his life. He had taken a meagre breakfast with the sole tenanted farmer on the estate before setting off in the only modest coat, shirt, and breeches he owned. His cloak now covered his father's remains, six feet beneath the fertile earth of the country churchyard.

Tom's chestnut mare snorted, eager to be down off the

rise and into the heart of the city. The stables near Shore-ditch were sound and dry, and the oats were soft, but she would have to share both with her penny-poor master that evening.

The muddy Edgware Road lay rutted from the morning rain, and lead to the great crossroads on the north road. A great swarm of people had gathered for the hangings taking place at Tyburn Tree: the triple-posted gallows supported by massive horizontal beams of oak. Twenty-four souls could hang at one time, and the spectacle had always disgusted Tom. He had recently passed the occupied gibbets, cages for the men and women hanged, that lined the route north from London with their squeaking warning of man's justice to the living and its inhumanity to the dead.

Tom rode down into the burgeoning crowd, following the carnival procession of hawkers, pickpockets, and the morbidly curious. He declined several opportunities to buy trinkets or an hour with a wart-ridden prostitute. Folios of scrawled last words from earlier hangings in the day were offered and also declined. The entire event, intended to be a warning against highway robbery, murder or the stealing of a few shillings, had developed into a loud, crass and volatile celebration of the macabre.

All life was here, and Death had a pew along with the wealthy in the erected stands. For the princely sum of two pounds, one could sit in comfort and watch the unfortunates dance the suffocating 'Tyburn jig' at the end of a rope. The route became congested, and Tom dismounted, before tying his horse to a nearby post. He threaded his lithe and lanky form through the crowd before he could go no further. The cart carrying the convicted appeared, parting the wave of eager and cheering spectators. Monday afternoon's entertain-ment had arrived in the bound forms of a poorly clad whore, a young and dashing cut-purse, and a richly dressed nobleman. The woman undressed and threw the remainders of what she wore to the masses, who cheered and fought to catch the souvenirs. They would sell for a pretty price, later on, relics of the day Bess Paxton met her life's end. Bess was lewd and bawdy but enjoyed her final few minutes of infamy. The crowd rejoiced to see her revel in her imminent destruction; courage, comedy, and tragedy are what they wanted, and Tyburn nearly always delivered.

The adolescent man in the cart egged her on and began a song of such debauchery that folk roared with laughter and acted out scenes from the song with drunken comrades. Tom was familiar with the first verse, which was set to a simple country tune, but blushed to hear the second. He was positively scarlet by the third verse.

The well-dressed man alongside looked on without emotion. He was in his late thirties and, surprisingly for the event, quiet and contemplative. The nobleman scanned the crowd, and the approaching gallows, as if searching for someone or something. There was no sign of fear or unease, as if he were travelling to a nearby shrine on a holy day. He caught Tom's eye for a moment and he felt awkward for the man's plight, so he nodded in compassionate respect. His pulse raced as the man closed his eyes and nodded back, in gratitude for the last kind soul with whom he would interact.

Tom stepped closer to the ring of people jammed around the giant three-legged stool of the gallows. The cart moved into position, and the draught horses manoeuvred their human cargo beneath the beam. There were many soldiers there to keep the peace amongst the lively crowd, and they held a small but secure area for the arrival of the executioner and black-robed minister, who would officiate for the hangings. They mounted the cart to great jeers from the mob in front. The official read out the charges, drowned out by the mocking and impatient crowd as the ropes were tensioned.

The brutish hangman fixed the length needed to choke the life slowly and cruelly from the three felons before him. Bess spat at the man, and he struck her on the face, before over-tightening the noose around her grubby fat neck. The crowd roared as she kneed him in the groin and leapt from the cart to end the ordeal on her terms. It was the final and most courageous thing she had ever done, and it worked. Her action shocked the crowd, and it had cheated them from the dreadful dance of her asphyxiation, now that her neck had snapped cleanly.

The young cut-purse cheered, and the masses responded to her heroism. The hangman, sweating profusely from the blow, draped the second noose around the man's neck.

'Go on, Billy,' shouted his lover, hoisting her dress to impress him one last time. 'Give us a song!'

The youth had a sweet voice, but a crude choice of song-book. The crowd cheered as he sang of whoring, drinking and gambling, but with a nod from the minister, the hangman kicked him from the raised cart. The song died instantly on his lips as the drop forced the air from his lungs. He attempted to gasp a final chorus, but the breath became too precious to waste, and too rare to process. He writhed and struggled, and Tom looked away. The multitude of everyday folk chanted his name, as men exchanged bets on the longevity of the poor man's futile efforts to stay alive.

Billy's vigorous jerks and twists became more muted, but he had just the strength for the last payment. He thrust himself forwards and swung like an acrobat from the neck. The lightly sewn stitch in his trouser pocket gave way, and a heap of copper pennies slid down his filthy cotton breeches and over his dirty bare feet. The soldiers parted, and a rush of children and family members gathered to steal the coins. They fought over the copper scraps, then collectively pulled down on the youth's dancing legs, hastening his end. The action was swift and merciful, and the man's motions died along with him. A few moments later, the children released and bolted, as a line of urine streaked down the man's legs. The official raised his hand in a token gesture of respect for the passing of the man's soul from this world to the next, and a hush descended as the crowd acknowledged it.

Tom turned around to see the finely dressed man freed from his bonds to remove the brocaded frock coat. The crowd gasped at the injuries to his wrists and neck inflicted during his tortured stay at the King's pleasure in Newgate Prison. The hangman tied his arms behind his back as the official read out his sentence.

'William Flint, I convict you of highway robbery, spying, and the murder of the Duke of Grantham upon this very road, three weeks ago in this, the year of our Lord 1747.'

The man remained circumspect in his silence. The crowd murmured and grew restless.

'Say something!' one cried.

'Speech!' shouted another.

He made his way, unaided, to the end of the cart and stood, closing his eyes to bask in the weak rays of the November sun.

Tom moved closer to study the man. He was impressive, despite his injuries. Well built and tall, like himself, but with the bearing of one suffering for a more significant cause. His shoulder-length brown hair, touched by an early frost of silver, draped and clung to his handsome face.

'I, therefore, sentence you to hang from the neck until you are dead,' continued the official. 'You have but a moment to repent of your sins in front of God and the honourable people of this county.'

There was much howling and jeering with the word 'honourable'. The minister pointed vainly at the soldiers to apprehend individual revellers who had taken to bending over and dropping their breeches in the cart's direction. The hypocrisy and irony were not lost on the educated masses in the pews, and they hooted with laughter, inflaming the minister further.

The man on the cart opened his eyes as silence descended.

'God save His Majesty, King George II. God watch over and protect my father and the good people of this realm.'

He caught sight of a hooded woman in the crowd and stared at her intently as he jolted sideways from the cart retreating beneath him.

'Vengeance is mine, sayeth the Lord, for myself and the Duke,' he shouted, towards the departing figure.

He stared straight into Tom's wide and naive eyes and took his last step in this world.

'Fortunes rise!' he cried as he dropped and swung clear of the cart.

The crowd cheered, but there was an air of discontent. There should have been a grander show of defiance, such as should have been forthcoming from a 'knight of the road' bold enough to rob and kill a duke. The man barely moved or danced a canto in his present misery, so they jeered. The speech was not heroic, and this was not entertainment.

Flint fiercely drew in a breath through his nostrils and was bombarded with all manner of unwanted fruit and rocks. He swung gently but defiantly, suffocating with such grace that Tom thought could not exist. The man jerked only once, and the stitches of his once-elegant breeches gave way to a cascade of worthless gravel.

The hangman and sergeant winked at one another, and the crowd laughed. Kinder souls perceived the horror of the situation; this man would suffer a long time. No payment was forthcoming, and no hands would pull down to speed his death.

Flint struggled to stay alive, his crimson face now heavily

veined. Rivulets of sweat and forced tears streaked down his cheeks as he sought to remain calm.

'Mercy!' cried several in the crowd, and the front row of onlookers repeated the call. They were witnessing bravery of another sort, one that they had not seen before. This was a meek and muted fearless action that contradicted the man's alleged crimes, and there was a growing tension; the soldiers looked over at the sergeant for reassurance.

'One only,' he shouted in resigned indignation, sensing the mood of the crowd. 'He killed a duke.'

'I'm not getting pissed on for rocks!' shouted a sallow-faced man.

'I want his coat if I am to burden him,' replied another, but a nearby soldier raised a cudgel to prevent his entry.

Tom locked his wide eyes on Flint as he pushed forwards, through the front row. Pity welled up inside him; he should do the right thing. He had, until a few weeks ago, been an emotional and fragile youth, but the ramifications of his father's death had hardened and numbed his sensitive and gentle nature. He strode forwards, hands raised, through the line of soldiers and advanced towards the dying man.

The minister restrained the hangman who moved to intercept, and Tom looked up into the noble and tortured face of the highwayman.

'May your fortunes rise, sir, in the life to come,' he whispered. He folded his arms around the highwayman's legs and pulled down, lifting his feet to add more weight. He did not hear the crowd, muted in its weak appreciation and jeering, but he listened to the man's breath tighten and restrict. A thin whine of lasting breath told Tom it would not be enough; the man was still too strong. Tom regained his feet, and Flint drew in a precious sip of air. Positioning himself beneath the highwayman's legs, Tom shouldered the man's bare feet and forced himself upright, lifting Flint into the air.

Flint rasped, as his restricted windpipe was forced open with the sudden availability of air.

Tom's legs trembled with the struggle of lifting the man, and he struggled to balance under the weight. In one swift action, like a troupe of acrobats he had once seen, he let the man's feet slip from his shoulders, clinging on and doubling the man's weight as he fell. Flint stiffened, and Tom made a final concerted effort to lend weight to the man's legs, squeezing the remaining air from his lungs.

Tom held his breath as the highwayman breathed out his last. He glanced up to see the man's face, a complex of emotions as life receded. Flint's eyes dilated as he turned in a final twitch to look at his side. Tom followed the terminal gaze. A bright object fell into his concealed lap from the man's formerly clenched fist. He had hidden it during the three miles from Newgate, and Tom turned his arm to gather it into his sleeve.

The minister raised his hand as the hanged man's arms hung limply at his side, and the crowd responded with muted and disgruntled chatter. The sergeant of the guard struck Tom on the shoulder, and he regained his feet and made to leave the circle. Only now, shaking and panting from the exertion, did he comprehend the enormity of what he had just done. The crowd booed as the hangman struck the limp form of the man several times to confirm his demise. Many surgeons, eager not to have the corpses damaged before their dissections, protested and made to restrain the sergeant's eager work. The hangman riffled through the swinging bodies for last-minute items, ripping off parts of clothing for sale to the highest bidder in the emptying pews. He paid particular attention to the highwayman and was disappointed to find him free of ornament. His eyes followed Tom as he retreated into the mass of onlookers, disturbed only by a disfigured woman rubbing the dead man's hand across her cratered face in search of a cure. Superstition was cheaper than a doctor's treatment, though not nearly as effective.

A chill and sudden wind rose in the circle. Dust and leaves whirled into the air, and the spectators shielded their eyes. It grew dimmer, with the setting of the sun, and people hurried away from the scene, crossing themselves for protection against the unnatural rising of the storm. Tom covered his eyes against the raging wind and made off towards his horse. A locket emerged from his cuff, and its cold metal case brushed his wrist. He stuffed it into his breast pocket, and clutched at his chest as if a burning or freezing object were branding him; he struggled to find the source of the sharp pain, and reached the empty stalls and posts a few painful minutes later.

The mare was missing.

Tom frantically scoured the road and the dissipating crowd through the dust and turbulent air. Apart from the distant draught horses, no other animal resembled his own.

He cursed his stupidity and cried out in misery through the storm that encircled the crossroads. A rage that he had never imagined before joined his consciousness, and he roared at the sky, consumed with thoughts of violence.

'Vengeance!'

The wind died as quickly as it had arrived and Tom sank to his knees, whimpering as he regained control. The nearby tavern sign squeaked mockingly as he examined his numb, shaking hands, planted in the road's filth.

He was destitute, alone, and had just ended a man's life.

<hr />

TOM SHIVERED IN THE DILAPIDATED BARN AS A DISTANT bell tolled for midnight.

He had pleaded for a place in the stables but narrowly

escaped a beating for his vagrancy. The stable-hand took pity and directed him to the half-roofed barn that overlooked the Kensington gravel pits, two miles to the east. He had taken a long drink of rainwater from a nearby cattle trough and settled down in the damp, derelict structure to wallow in the day's disastrous events. He thought of the several days' journey back to St Albans on foot.

Sleep was a near impossibility. The rain had stopped, and a stiff breeze had exposed a clear and chill moonlit sky. Tom was dry from crying, and the fiery rage that had consumed him at the crossroads was now nothing more than cold and lonely embers. How naive and foolish he had been. No doubt his poor horse was being sold miles away for little more than an evening's drunken revelry. He sat hunched in his wet clothes, gripping his knees and rocking with the memory of the highwayman's last gaze. He regarded his dirty and impoverished state and the prospect of not even being able to gain entrance to the solicitor's office in the morning. His anxiety rose, as did his heart rate, and the cycle of worry and internal circumspection began again.

An owl scared him as it flew in to roost. It interrupted the cyclical compulsive thoughts and he got up and moved around, desperate to get warmth into his frozen limbs. He had never known such cold or such hunger.

He thought of his father, working at his locksmith table, late into the night. Candles and firelight had always blazed cheerfully in the back room of the house when his nimble fingers worked the beautiful components. The boxes were usually destined for a wealthy or unknown client needing the most secure and ingenious security devices imaginable. He had delighted in his work, and Tom was always eager to have the latest or most difficult lock to pick, break open or test, before his father delivered it. They had been close since the death of his mother many years earlier, intimate in their obsession with the lock work at hand, and the small and growing smallholding they had tenanted. Tom thought of the warming fire, which had somehow gotten out of control during the fateful night he had been far away, courting unsuccessfully. He had returned to see the flames consume everything he held dear.

Tom touched his numb face, searching for the blistering that had healed several days ago. The vision of the inferno at the house came back in sharp relief to the freezing surroundings; the chill seemed to be deepening. He had endured the flames as long as possible, searching for his father, before the roof had fallen in and the neighbouring farm labourers had dragged him back screaming to safety.

A bite of cold struck his shirt pocket, and he scratched at the annoying sting, recalling the dead man's trinket. Shuffling over to a pool of moonlight that beamed in through a large patch of the open roof, he pulled out and examined the dazzling gold locket.

Tom studied the case; it was exquisitely engraved with a rose, entwined around a crucifix. He marvelled at the purity and clarity with which it sparkled in the moonlight between his finger and thumb. Whoever this had belonged to would have been sorry to be parted from it. He pressed on the clip, and the locket opened to expose, on one side, the face of a beautiful dark-haired woman, richly dressed. The other portrait was familiar: it was William Flint, the highwayman. It was a younger image, but the nobleman looked out handsomely. He slipped the locket over his neck, and the sudden biting sting of pain returned, this time from his breastbone where the golden curiosity lay against his skin. It was wholly consuming in its severity, and Tom struggled unsuccessfully to remove the locket before passing out from the acute agony of the experience.

'*WAKE UP. SOMEONE APPROACHES.*'

Tom awoke in the dark to the sound of the distant church bell tolling one o'clock. He was sweating and burned as though with fever. His senses were acute. The pungency of the rat droppings and the smouldering charcoal from the woodsmen half a mile away stung his nostrils. The scratching mice in the roof thatch and the preening of nightjars in the stubble field was magnified and near at hand. He saw more keenly in the darkness – sharp outlines of broken beams, the swirling knots within the wood, and the shadow crouching in the corner of the rafters.

Panic struck, and he recalled the memory of pain in his chest. He hurried to remove the locket and stuff it into his breeches.

'*It has served its purpose,*' whispered a voice that came from the direction of the hidden figure. '*You have opened it, and I have returned.*'

Tom left the locket around his neck and stepped back into a dark corner and looked up, terrified. He could see the details of the roof, but the shifting shadow in the rafters was unfathomable and formless.

'Who goes there?' he exclaimed, fearful like a cornered animal.

'*The man in the locket,*' came the reply.

The shadow drifted across the beams in the roof.

'Flint? You escaped the noose?' said Tom.

'*You know that not to be true,*' said the shadow. '*You yourself ended my life.*'

Flint slunk back to the corner in the ceiling and sighed.

'*Forgive me. I am still coming to terms with my current... predicament, but I am grateful for your mercy earlier today.*'

'You dropped your locket when you died,' said Tom,

lifting the chain and holding it in front of himself. 'Is that what you came back for?'

The shadow flitted to another oak beam, and Tom withdrew to the opposite corner.

'*I have no more use for any worldly trinkets, but perhaps the thug approaching from the pits sent to rob you of it will enjoy its beauty far more. Prepare yourself for my intervention; you are unarmed and will surely die if I do not manifest. I am here to protect you and repay my debt. Do you wish to live?*'

'Yes, but I do not have it in me to kill a man,' said Tom, picking up a section of broken pitchfork handle. He sneaked over to the window, looking out on the northern pits.

The shadow laughed, and Tom realised the contradiction.

'*No, but I do,*' said Flint.

'*It would seem our fortunes are not in the ascendant, despite your parting blessing to me. I desperately tried to keep the locket from you, a mere lad of seventeen summers, but fate intervened. It has strange powers, that I see now. I heard your rage in the street earlier when you cried out for vengeance. I awoke from a moment's eternity when you opened it.*'

Tom shook at the sudden realisation. 'I called you back?'

'*Death has reconsidered for the moment, but she has not forgotten, and never will. Pray it is only my soul she seeks.*'

Tom brandished the wooden stick awkwardly and peered out of the window. He watched as an approaching figure dismounted and quietly shifted from cover to cover, snaking its way ever closer to the barn.

'Who is it?' said Tom nervously.

'*Your horse-thief, and the man that helped put me in Newgate Prison for a crime I did not commit. Hush now and prepare yourself. This will be disconcerting for both of us.*'

What happened next was more than disconcerting. Tom's rapid heartbeat calmed, and he felt cold and disconnected. The chain of the locket seemed to constrict painfully and bite into his neck, as though feeding itself from his hungry veins. The gold tarnished and a growing shadow covered the surface. The sensation of something manipulating his body overwhelmed him, and he had the feeling of being 'worn', like that of a glove slipping over a living hand. Something was sliding into him, and while Tom was conscious, the spirit of Flint acted both independently and in tandem. Tom waved the remains of the wooden tool in front of his face to find out who held control.

'*Don't struggle. It will be harder for me to defend you,*' whispered the voice from inside Tom's head. '*Trust me now, not a word...*'

Tom watched as he uncontrollably tossed the handle into the open doorway and the approaching figure deviated towards it, drawing a wicked-looking knife. Tom climbed up onto an internal flight of horse-mounting steps and swung silently into the rafters. He had never been so agile, and he marvelled that his strength, even though another directed it, was capable of such a feat. His senses were acute, and he saw the wrapped figure slink into the barn and beneath the beam where he sat poised to spring.

'*Always from cover, from height, or behind...*' came Flint's voice.

Tom could sense what he intended, and the muscles in his thighs tensed. He dropped off the beam and onto the unsuspecting thug, knocking the wind and the knife from him. Tom rolled sideways and grabbed the blade as his assailant staggered to his feet and drew a pistol from his belt. Tom readied the knife for throwing and closed his eyes, realising the next move from Flint would rob him of the last of his innocence. From this moment forwards, he would know what it was like to have killed a man.

'*I can't see. Open your eyes for God's sake!*' screamed Flint, throwing the knife into the assailant who cried out in pain.

Tom opened his eyes and saw the man clutching his right shoulder where the knife had buried itself. The loaded flint-lock lay on the floor just out of reach. With Flint in control, he dived for the weapon and rolled into a crouch, aiming at the man who was struggling to pull out the blade. Tom's arm shook wildly.

'*Steady. Let go...*' came Flint's voice in his head.

Tom relaxed, and his arm steadied.

The man in the dirt squirmed in the dust as Flint took over Tom's ability to speak.

'*Did you kill her after you apprehended me?*' he asked.

'How can a mere boy fight like that?' said the thief.

'*Did you kill the noblewoman when you came for Flint?*' said the highwayman. Tom was powerless to overcome the conversation.

'Why would we have done that?' said the thief. 'She's the one in charge.'

'*In charge of what?*'

Under the control of Flint, Tom's arm raised the pistol to encourage further answers.

'The bloody Duke's murder, and that ridding of that nobleman this afternoon at Tyburn,' said the thief, raising a hand in pitiful defence.

'*She framed him?*'

'If that's what you call it. Her and that solicitor scheming to do them both away for jewels and things beyond my under-standing.'

'*You were there that night when the Duke was assassinated. You are part of Jeremiah's gang. I recognise you.*'

The thief grimaced as he tried to withdraw the knife. 'How the blazes would you know that?'

Tom struggled to regain control, to ask about the noble-woman's conspirator, and Flint fought back, but with a compromise.

'*What of this solicitor?*' Flint asked. '*Tell me, and I will let you live.*'

The thief held up his hand. 'I want nothing more to do with either of them,' he said. 'Pardew or something, away up near Shoreditch. He arranged the gang, and she was there to see that nobleman you smothered this afternoon copped for it. I'm only here for the locket – she wants it, and it wasn't on Flint's body.'

Tom regained control and blurted out, 'That's the solicitor I will see tomorrow!'

The thief snorted. 'You might have caught me off guard in a dark barn, but you won't beat his pet Spaniard. He's as quick with a blade as William Flint was, maybe quicker.'

Flint asserted his will. '*We'll be testing your theory; I guarantee it.*'

Tom could sense the feelings of betrayal, and there was a deep sharing of their experiences and emotions while they were joined.

The man pushed himself up onto his feet and staggered backwards. In one desperate act of agony and self-preservation, he ripped out the knife and hurled it in Tom's direction.

A twitch of the trigger and the pan of flash powder ignited. A second later, the charge fired.

The weakly aimed knife missed Tom, and over the extended flintlock, he saw the wounded man stagger and grab his chest where the bleeding hole emerged. The horse-thief fell back onto the earth, slithered for a moment in the dirt, and was still.

Tom was reeling with the thought of the man's death, despite having been in danger of losing his own life, and he dropped the pistol.

'Enough,' he said. 'Get out of me, spirit. I want no more of this.'

Flint surrendered, and the feeling of influence dissipated.

Flint left Tom with a brisk heartbeat, a heavy sweat and a sense of profound sympathy. The shadow moved away to screen the corpse.

'*Yes*,' said Flint. '*I know what you are going through, even though it was my hand that fired the fateful shot. It will stay with you, as did my first. You will be alive to remember it and atone for it if need be – that is the price of taking a man's life, even one so ill led and wretched as his.*'

'Who was he? How did he know I was here?' asked Tom.

'*Nobody in particular by the look of him, but paid by someone else to retrieve what they suspected you took. Whom did you speak with after my demise?*'

'No one,' said Tom, then recalled the tavern. 'Only the stable-hand...'

'*Foolish boy.*'

Tom realised his folly and sat down, head in his hands.

Flint's shadow shifted, and Tom flinched, still unsure.

'*I said foolish just now*,' said Flint, '*but without this knowledge and your courage, we cannot take vengeance, bring to justice the Duke's killers and gain my absolution.*'

'We?' said Tom. 'I'm not getting involved. I just killed a man and am destitute. The only inheritance I have is with a rascal solicitor that kills the nobility. Besides, look at the state of me; how am I going to get to see him at any rate?'

Flint shifted back to the beams and was for a long while silent.

'*Within this wretched building there lies a cache of clothes, ship's biscuits, and five silver florins. I will trade you these and the return of your horse outside for your help today and for a minor task once you have settled your affairs tomorrow. Do we have a deal?*'

The thought of taking off his soaked shirt and putting on dry clothes was very appealing. Even the prospect of a single mouldy biscuit within grasp was pure torture. 'Where is it, and I'll consider it,' said Tom.

'*Well said, Master...?*'

'Fielding, Thomas Fielding.'

'*The locksmith's son?*' he asked. '*You used to test the boxes I hear.*'

'Yes, but that is a secret. Only the Spymaster General is aware of the work my father did. How do you know about the lockboxes?'

'*Because I used to deliver them to their intended targets and act as security for their contents. Your father does a fine job of making them unpickable.*'

Tom closed his eyes and explained the accident that had taken his father's life, and his reason for being in London.

'*I am sorry for your loss. I wish I could speak with him, but he has passed over and out of my reach.*'

'You mentioned biscuits?' said Tom, returning to the thought of food.

'*The far window,*' said Flint, pointing to the black void facing the woodland beyond. '*Pull up the remaining part of the frame.*'

Tom moved over to the rotten piece of timber and rocked it back and forth. It came away cleanly like a rotten tooth pulled from a stony mouth. The thick double-skinned stonework of the gable end showed a narrow space and, glancing to see Flint's shade at the edge of the moonlit beam, he reached in and withdrew a cloth-wrapped bundle.

'One of your hideouts?' Tom unwrapped the clothing, a small clinking bag containing musket balls, coins, and three dusty but dry biscuits. He crunched through the brittle and tasteless meal despite the protestations of his teeth and gums.

'*A safe house for professional use, I served...*' Flint paused. '*I serve England, and its King.*'

'You were a spy?' asked Tom. 'They said you were a high-wayman, they say you killed a duke.' He put down the biscuits and lifted the clothes; they were dry and clean. A check for lice and the absence of body odour was all it took for him to undress. He paused, giving Flint an embarrassed glance.

'I give you an encounter with life after death, and you are coy about your manhood?'

Tom glanced down and shivered at his near-naked form. 'It's bloody cold, you know. Aren't you cold?'

'No, I burn for my absolution with your aid tomorrow as you promised.'

Tom pulled on the shirt and buttoned the breeches. They fitted well, but he had lost a fair amount of weight in the last few weeks, and the trousers hung from his pelvis rather than his waist. 'I didn't promise,' he said, reaching for a second biscuit, 'but what is it you want?'

'Your help via another binding tomorrow, to discover the facts. We will have vengeance.'

'Don't you mean justice?' said Tom, sliding down the wall into a crouch. 'And don't say "we" – I have problems enough.'

'Justice is for the living,' replied Flint, drifting from the opposite corner into a similar position. *'Let's take both, then – save England from those that seek her ruin, and restore you to your fortune. Now watch!'*

The shadow crept to the moonbeam and loomed man-sized at the end of the shaft of silver light. Tom regretted his words at once. He could make out the ghostly and indistinct form of the dead man, clothed it seemed in the regalia of his last appearance.

'Lend me but a little...'

The locket on Tom's chest pulsed like a heartbeat, its engraving glowing on its golden surface.

'Very well, but...' The case began to tarnish and cloud over as though being shrouded by darkness. The rose and crucifix glimmered beneath as it tightened on his skin. Tom panicked, but Flint held up a hand to settle his nerves.

'It is over. Look to the past,' he said and pointed to the trail

of moonlight dividing them. *'My salvation and your restitution. You will see that your predicament is but part of the whole. Both our fates changed that night.'*

Tom rubbed at his chest, now relaxed back from its brief constriction, and shuffled forwards on his knees. Tendrils of shadow coalesced along the beam of light, like dark steam rising into the frosty night. A coach and two horses in miniature formed and shifted as windblown smoke where the moonlight first flooded into the dusty and frosted earthen floor. The toy-like coach moved in front of him, and he gazed wide-eyed at the scene playing out before him from a great height. Other familiar features appeared, bordering the moonlit road that Tom recognised.

'That's the Great North Road near St Albans...'

'Shh... Watch closely.'

He scoured across the fields and lanes to see his house and the squat brick barn that had been his life. It was burning, and several riders were leaving the scene in a great hurry. They joined the road and raced down the wide thoroughfare to meet with others waiting for the coach to pass.

Tom lurched forwards into the moonlit fantasy, hovering over the building and swiping the shadow flames into disparate smoke.

'Father!' he cried.

'Wait! You need to trust me and quickly; do not disturb the image again. It appears your father's death was no accident – see how they carry the newly made lockbox, the same box the Duke was on his way to collect.'

'The gang burned down the house and killed my father for a box?'

'I think this was just mischief, on their way to rob and kill the Duke. I'm afraid your family business is widely known, even to the criminal classes. A sturdy box, especially one made impenetrable by your father, would be a valuable prize and worth a pretty penny.'

Tom stood upright and peered down as the scene unfurled.

Small patches of shadow formed into stands of fir trees, and several figures on horseback broke from the woodland and stopped the coach. They dragged out the passengers and shot them, followed by the coachman. Tom watched the miniature skirmish play out like an Olympian god, and saw the bodies dragged via roped horses to the woodland, powdering into formless smoke at the edge of the moonlit curtain. They carried the slumped forms of two others from the back of a horse and placed them into the empty coach.

'*The Duke and his counsel were already dead,*' said Flint, '*and here comes my betrayer.*' He pointed to a wisp of smoke that formed itself into the silhouette of the noblewoman, the very same that hung within the locket at Tom's chest.

'*Elizabeth, why?*' said Flint.

'You said you were a spy and that you knew the horse-thief that night,' said Tom, peering over the scene. 'Where are you in all this?'

Flint pointed further along the moonlit road to a slight rise. The scene was fading, but a single rider coalesced and shifted within a column of shadow. There was a bright blue flash from the rider's chest and a response from the locket that hung about Tom's neck; he clasped it, shutting out its bright light. A stand of trees blocked the road ahead, hiding the coach from his position, and the sound of tiny flintlocks fired into the sky spurred the lone horseman into action. The horse turned and raced down the slope towards the road. The ruffians nearest the coach were aware of the incoming rider, firing their pistols with slight puffs of shadowed smoke. They took up defensive positions and reloaded. A tiny figure took out and blew a hunting horn, revealing other riders who moved to intercept the incoming streak of shadow from the west. The bright blue point of light contained within pierced the darkness like a newly born star and Tom's locket blazed through his entire hand as if desperate to share in the proceedings.

The small and solitary figure of Flint gained the road and streaked along with it, firing two loaded flintlocks from his saddle straps. Minute specks of shadow raced ahead, striking and dismounting two men barring the road. They returned several ill-aimed shots before they drew their tiny swords and ran to meet him. Flint took out a massive blunderbuss from a stirrup-like quiver and fired, removing two men from their saddles at close range. His horse reared in panic, and it threw him. He grabbed a blade from the circling horse and fought off the remaining riders with a dazzling display of skill. The horse bolted and disappeared into the trees, and the light beaming out of the rider's shadowy form glowed a threatening garnet red.

'*Checkmate...*' said Flint.

'You?' said Tom. 'You didn't kill them, and you were trying to save them!'

The rider closest to the coach held up his pistol to the open carriage window and the whirling miniature of Flint stopped his killing but retained his sword.

Tom studied the scene like a battlefield general as the shadow next to him shifted and sighed. '*The Duke and his wife were already dead. Elizabeth and Pardew betrayed them and me.*'

The noblewoman re-emerged, held in pretence against her will.

'*They threatened to slit her throat if I didn't lay down my weapon. They wouldn't have touched her; I know that now.*'

The tiny figure cast aside his sword, and it vanished in a puff of smoke. Several of the gang rode off, taking the woman with them. She dismounted when out of sight of the road and gave instructions to the leader. The men by the carriage bound Flint as several other riders approached from a fork in the south, and Tom recognised, from the formation and discipline of their ranks, that they were soldiers from the barracks at St Albans. The redcoats approached the coach and, after a brief discussion, took Flint and rode away, leaving the rest of the murderous gang to ride north.

Tom looked back at the smoky form of the burning building to the north. The moon outside the barn faded behind a bank of cloud, and the image became challenging to perceive. The last image Tom saw was the miniature building with its roof close to collapse. A solitary young rider approached the inferno and dismounted. He ran into the house before being restrained by several figures, and he knew he was seeing his own past.

'Show me no more,' said Tom, but Flint had departed. The scene dissipated and Tom's burning home faded into the frosty air.

TOM DRAGGED THE DEAD THIEF INTO A NEARBY DISUSED well and rode back into Tyburn. He stole a half-sack of oats, a ripe cheese, and a cask of thin wine from the untended stables at the inn; a small payment in retaliation for conspiracy to murder, and a chance to test his frozen fingers on the woefully simple lock. The shadow of Tyburn gallows loomed overhead, and Tom pondered the two men dead at his hands. He seemed disconnected, as though the locket was working its strange magic again. Flint was innocent, and Tom had aided out of pity. The second man was killed in self-defence, and he accepted it.

He tugged at the golden case around his neck.

'Vengeance and justice,' he murmured, studying the locket and wondering if Flint's spirit could hear when not manifest. 'Before the sun sets today, we will have both.'

The silence continued as the horse and rider clip-clopped a further two miles to reach a dry copse of firs next to a narrow stream where they ate until they satisfied their shrunken bellies. Tom lay down and fell soundly asleep to the sound of the breeze in the resinous air, looking at the locket reflecting the sparkling light from the cold and innumerable stars.

HE AWOKE, WRAPPED IN THE EARLY MORNING DEW. HIS horse shivered nearby and tossed her head, waiting for food. They both drank from the nearby stream, and the steed nudged him playfully, eager to warm her stiff legs. Tom saddled up to make for Shoreditch and the offices of Pardew, the solicitor; today would see better fortune, and he could be on his way home. He tightened the stirrup strap and noticed the new breeches and the heavy blade, belonging to the dead man, that hung through his saddle loop. The evening came flooding back. He would have to deal with someone partly responsible for his father's death, not to mention the man behind the murder of the Duke of Sutherland. Pardew was also the target of the vengeful shade he had encountered, and who had saved his life. He wiped his nose in the chilly bracing air and brushed against the cold metal of the locket, recalling Flint's words in the barn.

'*We will have vengeance...*'

Tom resolved to deal with his affairs as swiftly as possible and leave matters beyond his station well alone. If the shade returned, he would seek an end to their arrangement at the nearest church; this was a spiritual matter, and he just wanted to get home. Tom turned his horse to the road, considering what to do with the locket. Perhaps he would throw it into the Thames and wash his hands of the entire affair in the dirty water of the river.

London loomed large after several miles and swallowed up the open sky. The narrow streets were difficult and busy to navigate, so he dismounted and led the mare to the street in Shoreditch.

Tall timbered offices overhung the thoroughfare, and he noticed a small but luxurious carriage with a grey palfrey and driver standing sentry. The well-clothed man took a pinch of snuff and eyed Tom as he tied his horse. He looked about and considered what to do with the heavy blade, knowing he couldn't leave it in the street. He felt sure the clerk in the office would allow him to remove it inside if he wore it openly. Tom lifted the sword in its cracked leather holder and tied it to the holstered belt he had inherited from the barn. Confidence returned, though this was only skin deep. The only instance he had wielded such a weapon was during a passion play in the town; he had later spent a week in bed from the deep gash to his groin during an ill-timed swing.

He knocked and gained entry.

Tom delivered his letter of introduction to the clerk who shuffled through the hall in front, beckoning him to wait until called. An open waiting room stacked with leather-bound books and papers made it look more like a deserted book-store, the silence only broken by the chiming of a clock. The doors swung open, and an impressive middle-aged woman with abundant auburn hair emerged, followed by a tall man in mournful legal attire. The solicitor bade a formal farewell and looked over at Tom who sat gaping in recognition. She was the noblewoman in the locket.

He grabbed at the gold case and stuffed it inside his shirt, but she stared back with malignant curiosity.

'Those are fine clothes, Master...?' she asked.

Pardew interrupted. 'Ah, the Fielding boy.'

The woman whispered in the solicitor's ear, and Pardew called through to his office.

'Gaspar, please escort my client to her carriage and see that she has everything she requires,' he said.

'Señor,' said a Spanish-accented voice.

The man who emerged was tall, dark and lean. He strutted past Tom, giving him a grunt of derision when he saw the crude sword at his side. Gaspar put his hand on his own finely wrought rapier and bared his yellow teeth. The Spaniard opened the doors to the street and followed the noblewoman out into the sunlight. Tom glanced through the dirty window to see them deep in talk. She was pointing back to the building, and Tom knew he was in trouble. He made for the door, but Pardew shut it and steered him through to his office.

'Your legacy, Master Fielding. I'm a busy man,' he said.

Tom waited for the opportunity to turn and bolt through the door but the Spaniard returned, grim-faced, and barred the way.

'If you please,' said Pardew, 'it seems we have much to discuss.'

The clerk closed the doors and Tom knew a trap was being sprung.

Pardew offered him a seat, and Tom sat down, hampered by the long sword and making a mess of the simplest of tasks. A look from the solicitor silenced the Spaniard, who had burst out laughing. Pardew pulled out a bundle of documents from his desk. The tall swordsman bent down and whispered in his master's ear before wandering over to the marble fireplace to stroke a delicately wrought box. Tom knew the object, and its mechanism; the last and greatest strongbox his father had made before the fire.

'You are here to discuss the transfer of your father's assets, as beneficiary and sole heir,' said Pardew. 'Unfortunately, the law is specific about my role in allowing a known felon to do so.'

'I'm no felon!' said Tom, standing upright.

'No?' said Pardew. 'Then how do you come to wear the sword of one man that did not report this morning, and the clothes of another that died like a dog at Tyburn yesterday?'

Tom was out of his depth.

'You are a thief,' continued Pardew, 'and likely a murderer, or accessory to one. There is also the matter of the locket you stole from Lady Elizabeth.'

'I stole no such thing,' said Tom, shaking with fear. 'It dropped from William Flint at his hanging yesterday.'

'Flint?' Pardew laughed. 'You think that will wash with the judge? You are likely in league with him or picked his corpse last night. I should know, I helped put him there.'

Tom was aware of a strange sensation, emboldening his responses. He glanced over at the Spaniard, who kissed his fingers and patted the lockbox.

'That's my father's box – the one your gang stole before they torched my home, murdered my father, and killed the Duke on the north road. Get your filthy hands off my property.'

The Spaniard reached for his sword, and Pardew held up a hand.

'*No!* Not here, Gaspar. Tell my clerk to fetch the thief-takers to apprehend this highwayman's apprentice.'

Gaspar spat and nudged past Tom, out of the room.

'Now, Master Fielding,' said Pardew, 'it's time to haggle for your life. Did you torture my little ruffian last night for that information? I marvel you could strike a rabbit, let alone despatch a man of his talents.'

'You sent him to kill me, didn't you?'

'My noble associate and I hate loose ends; I'm sure you

understand.' He looked over at the box. 'It's beautiful, isn't it? Hides all of my secrets securely.'

Gaspar came in and barred the escape from the room.

'He's gone, Mr Pardew,' said the Spaniard, cricking his neck and cracking his knuckles, expecting an order to injure, maim or kill. He would beat this boy with one flick of his blade, but he resolved to play with the gangly youth until his master grew tired and ordered the killing and removal of the body.

'The locket, Master Fielding, if you please, then we can review your present situation. The judge might change the sentence from hanging to life in the colonies, especially if you will be so gracious as to represent me as your father's beneficiary.' Pardew held out one hand, and in the other, he dipped a quill, ready for Tom's signature on the document before him.

Tom stared down at the hastily drawn document, realising his doom. Death at Tyburn like a felon, or back-breaking servitude in the fields of the Americas; he would never return to his home either way and escape from the building was impossible.

He shook, knowing that his life was at an end. His courage was not enough to surrender to the hangman's noose, and he reached for the locket within his shirt.

The stab of sudden ice from the gold case caused him to cry out, and Pardew signalled for his bodyguard to take the necklace by force.

Tom clutched in agony at his chest, unable to separate his fingers from the locket. He was conscious of his other hand drawing the sword, and the voice of Flint resounded in his head.

'*I rise!*'

The Spaniard's eyes sparkled in anticipation of a duel and he drew the wicked blade at his side in response.

A sudden and indeterminable wind from within the room cascaded the papers and blew the quill from Pardew's hand. Gaspar halted, unsure of what was causing the air to move in such a fashion. Pardew crossed himself, moving aside towards the mantelpiece and away from the source of the disturbance.

Tom's pain stopped as swiftly as it had arrived, and he withdrew his hand to discover the image of the crucifix and the rose branded into his palm. The feeling of being worn like a glove returned, and he recognised the shade of Flint entering his body just in time to parry a heavy blow from the Spaniard.

Its impact spun him around, and Gaspar sheathed his weapon; he threw a wired garrotte around Tom's neck, pulling it tight. It cut into Tom's throat so quickly that he flailed, trying to get his fingers beneath its sharp and tightening bite to get precious air back into his lungs.

'*Fool! Not the wire – the fingers, grab his fingers and break them. You have little time!*'

'I... can't... breathe...' Tom screamed internally, dropping his sword and grabbing at his assailant's fingers. He found the little finger of his enemy's left hand and twisted it sideways. There was a grunt, and Tom threw himself back into the desk, causing the grip to lessen.

'*Elbows!*' Flint commanded.

Tom gasped for air and swung his elbows into the soft part of the Spaniard's chest. The sensation of being worn was complete, and he could now defer to Flint's greater experience and prowess. He perceived Flint's spirit was gaining strength and familiarity within him.

Tom tensed his legs, and he lurched forwards, throwing the attacker over his back. Gaspar hissed as he made to get up from a set of books.

'*Now you know how I felt yesterday*,' Flint said. '*Pick up your sword, by the corner, quickly! I don't want to die twice, not to that clown at any rate.'*

Tom turned and ran for the sword, scooping up the heavy hilt. 'How can you joke about death when I'm about to join you?' Tom said internally, rubbing his throat to check for blood and seeing the swordsman behind draw his long rapier. Tom glanced at the crude blade in his hands.

'I can't use this; I don't have the skill!'

His hand tightened on the hilt, and he took a defensive stance.

'No, young rabbit, but I do...'

There was a brief and cursory clash of blades, and Tom's right hand fluttered and flicked the lighter blade aside. Gaspar took a step back, confused by the inexperienced man's sudden skill with a sword. The young pup in front of him could barely lift the weapon moments ago.

'Change hands, Tom.'

'But I'm left-handed.'

'That's nice,' said the shade. *'But I'm not.'*

Tom tossed the hilt to his other hand, and the sense of confidence and expertise manifested. The arrogance infuriated Gaspar and he deftly feigned a cut to the head. Tom was too late to recognise it for what it was and whirled away just in time, receiving a nasty slash to his upper cheek.

'Let me do the thinking!' said Flint. *'I saw that coming.'*

The Spaniard made a more determined attack, but Tom repelled and replied with a lunging riposte of his own. He marvelled at the deftness, strength, and speed in his sword arm. It was like watching Gaspar perform in slow motion compared with Flint's speed and skill.

'You were a superb swordsman,' he exclaimed to Flint.

'I am a superb swordsman,' came the reply. *'I hope you're watching this; I can't be around to save you every time you get into trouble.'*

Tom gained the initiative and now parried securely and confidently. Something was empowering and guiding him, and it was exhilarating.

'*Yes, you feel it, the thrill of the fight, the exhilaration of knowing you can best this imbecile,*' said Flint. '*At which point you will lose and get the point of his left-handed short blade, that you have failed to notice.*'

Tom glanced down and saw the other weapon, designed to disengage his own. Two swords against one. 'What do we do now?' he said, flicking his blade forwards to keep the attacker at a distance.

'*Normally a flintlock to the face, but this time we must do it the hard way. You will need to take the initiative; it's getting difficult for me to stay with you,*' Flint said.

Tom was gaining control, which was disconcerting. The sword was heavy, and his extended arm shook.

'*He's not bad,*' said Flint, '*but this sword is blunt except for the tip. Trust me now; this might sting a little...*'

'What do you mean...' started Tom, concerned by the thought of further injury. The Spaniard circled his rapier and held the short sword, ready to disarm any strike. Tom trod on his own foot as he retreated, dropping his weapon as he struggled to avoid falling backwards.

Pardew shrieked out from the other side of the room, 'Kill him, you fool!' Gaspar saw his chance and rushed at Tom, who dropped to his knees.

Tom's strength and courage returned. '*Shut your eyes, Tom. You need not see this. He's close enough for me to deal with...*'

Tom obliged but felt both his hands guided by the shade. He grabbed the sword's dull cutting edge beneath the hand-guard and sprung up, from his haunches, between the two blades of the swordsman upon him. The pommel struck the Spaniard fully under the chin, with the force of a sprung hammer, breaking his jaw and sending him reeling back. He screamed and grabbed for his face, still bearing the weapons. Years of training had not dulled his instinct, but his chest lay open and unprotected.

Tom spun his sword, feeling the wet blood of the cuts in his palms drip down the hilt, and he drove the horse-thief's blade into the heart of the second-best swordsman in England alive, or dead.

Gaspar collapsed, bloodied froth issuing from his mouth. He dropped his weapons and fell backwards, ripping the hilt from Tom's hands. Tom opened his eyes to see the Spaniard clutch at his chest, then look up at the lad of seventeen summers in disbelief. He marvelled at the deception and then died.

Pardew whimpered and whined now that his protector was dead. Tom turned to address the man cowering against the fireplace.

'You kill me, and you'll hang! The thief-takers are on their way,' squealed Pardew.

Tom replied without aid from Flint. 'My associate seeks vengeance, and I pursue justice for my father; it's up to you now, Mr Pardew, to decide whether it is you who hangs or travels to the colonies.'

'What associate?' said Pardew, feeling for the lockbox.

'The man who you framed for the Duke's murder, William Flint.'

'Flint?' said Pardew. 'He's dead, you fool. Lady Elizabeth and I saw to that. You are his pupil, after all!'

Tom looked down at his cut palms and wiped them down his breeches. He picked up the Spaniard's garrotte for dramatic effect, knowing he did not have the power in his hands or the upbringing to kill a man in such a fashion. Pardew withdrew to the desk, clutching the box.

'*Let me do it. You can close your eyes again,*' said Flint.

'No,' said Tom, out loud. 'I will not go down that road.'

'*We have a brief time for vengeance and to escape,*' said Flint. '*Even now the thief-takers bring redcoats.*'

'He must grant my inheritance and pay for his crimes under the law,' replied Tom. 'Out of me, spirit. No more.'

Pardew watched in confusion as Tom argued with himself like a madman. Seeing an opportunity, he bolted for the door, clutching the box to his chest.

Tom felt the shade slip from his body, and pain returned. His hands and cheek burned with the cuts and his arms boiled with lactic acid from the exertion; Flint had been shielding the sensations from him, but he was no longer within Tom.

He was between the door and the petrified form of Pardew.

'*Traitorous scoundrel!*' said Flint, as Pardew recognised the full horror of the thing barring the door.

'No, no!' cried Pardew. 'This cannot be – you're dead!'

'*You will shortly join me, and Lady Elizabeth...*'

Tom wrapped his bleeding hands with torn strips from the window curtains. He scooped up the papers from the floor, searching for his father's name on the document that would release his estate.

'Sign this,' said Tom. 'Sign it, and I will vouch for your soul at the inquest.'

There was a loud thump on the outside door that the clerk had locked on his way out. 'Open up,' cried a voice. 'We are here to apprehend the felon.'

Pardew took heart from the soldiers' arrival.

'Never,' said Pardew, shaking with the fear of Flint's shade looming over him. 'You have no proof, and you have no key.' He looked down at the box confidently.

'*Then let me give you a taste of oblivion, and what lies beyond...*' said Flint.

Flint faded, and Tom knew from Pardew's expression that

he was experiencing the sensation of being bound to the spirit's will. He dropped the box and screamed, trying to cover his eyes, and tearing at invisible forms in front of him.

'No! Send them away! Mercy!' screamed Pardew.

There was a repeated thump from beyond as the soldiers became impatient.

'*No mercy for you, not even from all those you sent to the gallows, innocently and unjustly. They are legion, Pardew, and they wait for you...*'

'I'll sign it! Make them go away!'

'*You will sign and then confess...*'

'Yes, anything. Release me, I beg you.'

Flint relented, and Pardew stared with madness at the dissolving forms. Tom presented the document and the quill, and he signed it without hesitation.

The outside door burst from its hinges, and the soldiers raced into the antechamber. They hammered on the internal panelling, demanding entry to the office.

'Lady Elizabeth has the key,' murmured Pardew. 'She will not release it willingly. It has our agreement...'

Tom picked up the box, the last thing his father had made and handled before he died. The delicate tracery of the silver and gold lines was familiar, raised above the dark exotic wood. He knew it was unpickable, even by him.

He also knew the other way to open it.

'*Hurry!*' said Flint. '*We need the letters inside.*'

The doors bulged with the weight of the men banging from the other side as Tom gripped the sides of the box.

He felt for the familiar lines and pushed them slowly from their routine positions. He released them, and the tiny springs returned them to their former state. There was a click as the delicate mechanism inside responded. He turned the box over and repeated the movements with his fingers pushing against the intricate filigree of the lines. The device completed its unlocking, and the lid rose gently to display a bound stack of letters, written in a woman's hand, and several items of jewellery with the Duke's symbol upon them.

'*Remember what has passed between us,*' said Flint, fading into the flocked wall-hangings, '*and what will come to pass if you fail to confess...*'

Pardew nodded and released the bolts from the door. Four redcoats with fixed-bayonet rifles strode in accompanied by the thief-taker. They were greeted by the sight of the dead Spaniard, awash with blood. Tom stood, open box in hands covered with bloody bandages. Pardew stood, trance-like, his mind shattered from what he had experienced.

'Arrest the boy,' said the thief-taker, 'and see to Mr Pardew.'

The redcoats advanced, but it was Pardew who spoke first.

'The boy is innocent of any crimes here. The man you seek lies dead over in the corner.'

'How so? What transpired here? They sent me to apprehend a boy connected with the highwayman, and the Duke's murder,' said the official.

'The contents of the box will explain everything, including my role in the entire affair.'

Pardew rose and gave Tom a long last look.

'Tell your... associate, I will abide by our arrangement,' he said to Tom, as they led him away.

'You did this?' said the thief-taker, pointing at the Spaniard. 'In self-defence?'

'He attacked first when I discovered Pardew was partly behind the murder of the Duke.'

'He paid William Flint?'

'No, Flint had nothing to do with it,' said Tom. 'The letters outlining the plot are in here.'

Tom handed over the box, and the man signalled for the

returning soldiers to remove the Spaniard's body. 'Is that your horse out there?'

'Yes,' said Tom. 'I will accompany you and testify against both Pardew and Lady Elizabeth. The Duke's stolen belongings are beneath the papers.'

'The noblewoman? You accuse her of conspiracy to murder?'

'It's all in the letters. You'll find it was Jeremiah's gang that assassinated the Duke, but it was Pardew and the noble who arranged it.'

'If what you say is true, then I have some explaining to do with the Marquis, William Flint's father.'

Tom took off the locket. 'Take this to him,' he said, 'from one that sought to clear his name.'

The thief-taker opened the locket and whistled. 'There's a tale to tell here, and you need to come willingly to explain your role in it.'

'Agreed,' said Tom, 'though I could use a surgeon to help with my wounds.'

'I will arrange it.' He looked over at the soldiers lifting the corpse. 'When all this is settled, I may have a role for someone with your skillset.'

Tom raised the paper document outlining his inheritance. 'I have a future now, rebuilding what Pardew and his gang destroyed.'

The man wrapped the locket in his handkerchief. 'Let us hope this lays his soul to rest, then,' he said.

'My thoughts exactly,' said Tom, glancing around the empty room.

The thief-taker ushered him out of the building and into the weak sunlight of the morning. Tom untethered his horse and followed him as he instructed the soldiers to part the sizeable crowd that had formed.

Free of the locket, he only encountered Flint once more.

THE DAY OF THE HANGING DAWNED CLEAR AND BRIGHT. The December crowds, buoyed by the impending prospect of Yule, were more significant than in previous days. They arrived to see something special.

A noblewoman would hang today.

Tom reluctantly returned to London at the bequest of the Marquis, who was eager to repay his son's pardon. He sent his stonemason and carpenters to aid in the rebuilding and refurnishing of Tom's home and also offered several orders for lockboxes, and a covert meeting with the spymaster about future commissions. He offered him a seat in a row reserved for the gentry, but Tom left a respectful distance between himself and Flint's father.

Lady Elizabeth Montague arrived dishevelled in the horse cart alongside other unfortunates doomed to hang. Her once-beautiful gown now ripped and torn – delicate pieces sold off to pay for last comforts during the sleepless nights in Newgate Prison.

Pardew was not amongst them. If he survived the treacherous Atlantic storms, he would soon arrive in the Americas for a life of toil alongside the other convicts. Tom had appealed his capital punishment, and they commuted the sentence to transportation when the letters revealed that Pardew was but a pawn in the entire affair. Even now, the gang and other political rivals of the Duke were being hunted for his murder.

The large number on the cart did not receive the usual courtesies, and the men and women died in quick succession, kicked from the mobile wooden platform. The noblewoman struggled to maintain her dignity and shook with fear, and the intense cold. They placed the noose around her neck, and she looked out wildly, then focussed in horror upon Tom, or one next to him. Tom glanced sideways towards the Marquis and the space between them. He was aware of Flint's presence, though not his form.

'*Yes*,' said Flint, '*death approaches, and she sees me.*'

Tom watched as she screamed in recognition, 'Forgive me!'

The cart slid away, and she fell, swinging wildly until the children ran in to tear at the rest of her finery in last payment for their groping hands upon her tattered stockings.

'Justice or vengeance?' whispered Tom, sensing Flint fade as the noblewoman breathed out her last.

'*Justice in this world, but vengeance in the next...*'

THE MOST MAGNIFICENT
MENKA

M enka transformed me into a rabbit for my act of
charity, and I was caged for three days.

I was used to the experience by then. The first time
Menka changed me was my fault and was disconcerting,
though in truth, returning to my adolescent form was the
worst part. A rabbit does not realise what's happening and is
ill-prepared for the event. I don't recommend the ordeal
unless you have the cash, which is what the travelling magician and we, his apprentices, relied upon for our livelihoods. I
mention 'apprentice', but we were little better than servants
and he taught us little, much to his own cost and the cost of
the local community along the Camino de Santiago. The
pilgrim route from Bilbao to the shrine of St James at
Santiago de Compostela was our lifeblood during that swel-
tering summer of 1870. I wish I had never seen his act, but
then I would never have met Alasne.

I'd first encountered him setting up in the town plaza,
alongside the travelling band of acrobats, artists and entertainers that played for pilgrims in stops along the route. He
was a tall, olive-skinned man, rumoured to be Egyptian by

birth, richly clad in royal purple, with thinning grey hair and a hook-like nose. He ticked all the boxes for my first sight of a stage magician. Alasne, his apprentice, was a girl of about my age and she looked hungrily at my basket of oranges for sale, the first of the season.

The wandering band erected a strong wooden platform. Upon it and to the rear was a painted screen depicting mythical beasts and mysterious astronomical symbols, which afforded a theatrical backdrop to the passion plays, acrobatics and displays of strength and agility. It rustled like a gigantic flag in the chilly winds, and I could perceive there was a central slit to gain access to the narrow space beyond. The large blank wall immediately behind was a perfect and secluded spot for performers and clowns to make their way onto the stage.

It also provided the screen for the routine of 'The Most Magnificent Menka'.

With the departure of the minstrels, Alasne lit the candle lamps at the platform's edge, and the feeling of anticipation rose in the gathered crowd. The finale never disappointed.

Alasne blew a small silver trumpet and signalled for quiet. Her introduction on the powers of her master was well rehearsed and, as I realise now, understated.

'LADIES AND GENTLEMEN,' SHE SAID IN A RAISED VOICE, 'you are about to see and experience things beyond your wildest imaginings!'

'Have you met my wife, then?' shouted a drunkard from the back of the crowd.

There was much laughter from the villagers. Alasne ignored the heckler and continued with professional grace.

'He has performed his magic across the sundering seas, to kings and queens, to paupers and popes...'

'And now he's here in this dump!' roared a farmer, much to the amusement of the locals.

'Beware, I urge you all, the magnificent Menka is a magus of tremendous power and wisdom. He sees all and has unlocked the secrets of the third plane of transcendence.'

There were murmurings and nods of respect from the villagers and pilgrims; I include myself in their ignorance of what a 'third' plane was. It sounded impressive, even though we were expecting only a sleight of hand routine, and maybe a few doves from the sleeves of his velvet stage robes.

We were wrong.

Menka ascended the makeshift stage carrying a crystal ball and several alchemical pieces of equipment. The crowd descended to a hush. He began a monologue on the arcane, and the power that coursed within him. Menka was an eloquent and commanding speaker, honed through decades of performance. Alasne joined him on the platform, carrying his heavy bound books. Her beauty mesmerised me under the flickering lamp lights of the stage, and I felt enchantment for the first, but not the last, time for free. She caught my appreciative eye and winked at my blushing face.

There was a short act involving the transmutation of objects, which pleased the crowd, despite their lack of faith in the magic – I recognise now in hindsight – I was witnessing. A belt from a pilgrim transformed, in a flash of lit powder, into a silken scarf bearing the blessed image of St James. The astonished recipient did not see the belt ever again, but as the scarf was more valuable, he was content, though inconvenienced for the rest of his journey by the loose fashion in which he wore his trousers.

Menka's reputation had preceded him, and several of the crowd had witnessed the show before. The movement of the travelling performers and the pilgrims often overlapped, and the travels from one end of the holy route to another meant they would encounter each other on their return. A second viewing allowed the mind to consider how the man was creating the illusion unfolding behind the screen.

A round of applause signalled the end of the first act. Alasne lit several braziers that gave off coloured and scented smokes. Exotic spices and fragrances filled the air and blew across the market square. The clouds parted, and the waxing moon illuminated the stage, looking down like a shining spectator, waiting for the magical second act to begin.

Menka covered his eyes with a black cloth and primed the crowd in a quiet voice. The onlookers strained to hear and settled into silence.

'Who among you is the bravest?' said the magician. 'Man, woman or child?'

There was a murmur as he scanned the gathering before him, blindfolded.

'Who will dare the portal of change? The cost is one escudo to unlock the magic of the ancients and to ensure a full recovery. Who among you is the bravest?'

The villagers forced their hands into their pockets with the mention of one escudo, a goodly sum especially at the start of harvest. They had, of course, donated a few pesetas to the bowl in a polite and expected offering for the evening entertainments, but they waited for a pilgrim to raise a hand so they could witness the rest of the show. The holy travellers seemed to have the same idea, having spent their modest coin on trinkets and sacred tokens at the shrine of St James, two days earlier. Paying once for entertainment was sufficient, paying again was highly unusual.

Alasne scanned the crowd, searching for anyone with a hand raised. It was tough in March for those tending the land, and the pilgrims were thin and far between. The busy Christmas period was over, so too the sizeable crowds in the bustling cities along the coast with their wealthy merchants.

Whatever the group and whatever the season, Menka did not alter his price.

The crowd stood immoveable, looking around at their fellow men, nudging and prodding them into a reckless expense for the entertainment of others. Sensing the mood of the crowd, she whispered in Menka's ear, and he nodded. She searched the gathering for me, and we locked eyes.

'One only,' she said, 'to appease the spirits and show the power of the magnificent Menka; one only for free.'

Hands shot up from the front row with the offer of something 'free', and men goaded those with their hands still in their pockets to do the same.

She pointed in my direction, and Menka looked out, still blindfolded. He beckoned to me and addressed the crowd.

'The bravest among you here tonight is barely a man,' he boomed. 'Come and witness the power at my command, young master.'

I should have bolted and spent my life ridiculed within the village as a coward, but hindsight is always a precious commodity.

The men pushed and jeered at me until I made my way to the steps of the platform. Alasne smiled as she took my hand, and I knew the nature of sudden and unforgettable first love. She led me to the screen as Menka continued his preamble to the display of mystical forces he would conjure and tame. The crowd seemed larger in front of me than I had expected, and Alasne led me beyond the screen. There was barely enough room against the wall to turn, and I bumped into the few stage props from earlier parts of the show. At either end, I saw the muscled forms of the two strongmen prohibiting entry to the narrow slits between the screen and the wall.

I glanced out nervously to see Menka prancing about the stage and calling on ancient deities to transform the brave soul beyond the screen into its natural spirit form for all to see. Alasne manoeuvred me into position, out of sight of the expectant crowd. She held up a finger to her lips for me to be quiet, putting her arms around me. I confess the arousal and unexpected good fortune took my breath away. Menka began an incantation, and I glanced one last time at my fellow farm-workers laughing and pointing at me.

When the screen was parted in an instant by the muscular strongmen, the farm-workers laughed no longer.

They raced to the back of the crowd who surged forwards with amazement. The wall beyond was bare, and the farm boy I once was had vanished. Alasne held me in her arms, and I nestled into her intoxicating perfume. I didn't care about being the fool, or whatever was causing the pilgrims' purses to open in such a frantic fashion.

Not until I realised I wasn't being held. I was being carried.

Alasne put me down, and I hopped around the wooden platform, closely monitored by the magician taking in the applause and greedily eyeing the coins held up in front of him.

'Behold the rabbit!' he bellowed. 'Innocent, trustworthy and naive – the boy's true form!'

The crowd rejoiced and marvelled at how the switch could have happened in so short a time. Several looked beneath the stage, convinced that a trapdoor was the answer. There was no such trickery; I was a rabbit. It took a little time to realise, but it was the lack of forward vision that told me things were not as they should be. My eyes, firmly rooted to the left and right of my head, showed the sides of the stage most clearly until I turned to watch the animated crowd cry and holler in my large and sensitive ears. I did not have the chance to investigate the large whiskers in front of me before I smelled the approach of Alasne, who scooped me into her arms once again. She returned with me to stand, back to the wall. The strongmen pulled across the screen, and the queasy sensation of transformation returned. I returned to the form of my birth and looked into her emerald eyes. She kissed me for the first time, and I made to hold her tightly when the screen withdrew. We stood together only for a fleeting moment, the happiest of my life, before the crowd erupted into praise for my safe return and the speed of Menka's illusion. The farm-hands stared, amazed, for a different reason; the timid farm labourer away from his home for the season had picked the best-looking fruit imaginable.

She led me from the stage as several pilgrims and villagers lined up for their turn. I glanced back to see Alasne still looking in my direction before the impatient Menka scolded her, sensing the smell of eager patrons and their coin.

The transformations continued. The blacksmith's wife, ever quick to spend money, became a mouse. It was some time before she was recovered from the crowd and restored. The comedy of the act lay in the animal form revealed. The villagers howled as the personality of the paying volunteer matched with the animal revealed, often only confirming what they already knew. One thing was for sure, Menka was a rich man, at eight escudos for an evening's work. I wondered how many he would transform during the summer and harvest months, let alone the big Christian festivals later in the year.

I enjoyed the rest of the performance, and clung to every intermittent glance from Alasne, while my comrades poked and slapped me in mutual respect and envy. The show ended, and folk sought the secret from those who had paid for the privilege; unfortunately, they were equally baffled and could provide no logical opinion. What was clear, though, was that many of them would never eat rabbit, pig, or sheep again.

I resolved to speak with Alasne later while assisting with the tidy up and breaking down of the stage, but she would only hold my hand and tell me she would be gone in the morning and that such things were best left as they were.

'I might come back in September?' she said hopefully, and my heart sank.

I returned to my shared hut after midnight and resolved that I would pick no further fruit that spring.

———————

THE MORNING WAS WET, AND I PACKED MY MEAGRE belongings and a spare change of clothing into my travelling bag. I left a scrawled note on the plaster above the straw-stuffed mattress and left my sleeping companions to their harvesting lives.

My parents would not expect me to return to the distant town on the coast until the autumn. By that time, I hoped to be back in the same area if life on the road did not turn out to be the experience I expected. I resolved to send a letter at the first opportunity, provided the travelling troupe would take me on, even for menial tasks. To be close to Alasne was all I wanted.

I found them gone from the village and tracked their heavy carts and covered wagons to the line of cedar trees on the hill many miles to the east. My heart rose, knowing I would see the distant towns beyond.

Visiting Ponferrada, León, maybe even as far as distant Pamplona and the mountains of the Pyrenees, drew me on and I found the troupe resting their horses beside a stream. It surprised them to see me, none more so than Alasne, who was washing a dirty shirt in the crystal water of a shallow pool.

They welcomed me, and I worked for board and lodging, but remained apart from the women, as was their custom. Menka maintained a close eye on any interaction with Alasne and scowled, calling me 'rabbit' despite knowing my actual name. I learned he had bought her when she was a child, though she was glad of the opportunity to be away from the hovel and abuse of her earlier life.

I fell in with the carpenter who built the stage and also played the lute. In time, he taught me how to do both. We travelled, performed and hunted in the wild for game, though I could never afterwards eat rabbit, having been one. Life was intoxicating, and I soon grew in confidence and talent to perform new routines, often ones I had invented and worked on myself. The finale, however, belonged to Menka, and the troupe owed their talented and diverse livelihoods to him, playing second fiddle to his illusions and magic. The topic of his money never arose, and I saw none of it shared between the other members of the troupe. He was his own man, and stayed apart, studying his books and strange maps, and did not engage in talk or laughter around our campfires in the wild. He kept Alasne close to him, and we had to be creative in our trysts and secret meetings. When he caught us, it was days before she was allowed any freedom again. I taught her how to read and write, much to the annoyance of Menka, and I read her the letters I sent home.

In all my time with the troupe, I could not figure out the secret behind the magic he performed. The incantations seemed to change nightly and were in an unfamiliar and guttural language that made mimicry impossible. The other members accepted that he could do miracles, and I knew myself, as the promoted chief carpenter, that there was no trapdoor or trickery involved.

I asked Alasne about the animal forms he would conjure, as they seemed to revolve around a restricted palette of docile creatures.

'What if the person's spirit conjures a lion or a tiger?' I asked naively.

'Don't be silly,' she replied. 'He only ever does a handful of creatures, ones that we can easily and safely manage. You wouldn't expect me to cuddle an elephant, would you?'

'So there's no magic in the choice,' I asked, 'just a random decision for comic effect?'

I felt aggrieved by Menka's first impression that I was timid and small, though being turned into a donkey was a lot worse.

'Yes,' she said, sneaking into my arms, 'I was the one who suggested the form. You have turned out to be trustworthy, innocent and naive after all.'

Her honesty struck me, and she twitched her nose, mockingly, inches in front of my own.

'I'd turn you into a toad,' I said, then kissed her before she had the chance to strike.

———

THERE CAME A DAY WHEN I ENTERED MENKA'S SERVICE, albeit part-time when the crowds were large enough. Alasne had burned her hand over the fire while trying to mix one of his experiments: an unsuccessful attempt to turn cheese into gold. Her hand blistered, and she winced while dressing for the show. The small and lucrative market town close to Burgos was full, and Menka realised his assistant was incapable of performing. She could not collect the coins for the evening's performance or hold, restrain and reclaim the creatures that the paying public would become.

Menka was also suffering from an illness and had been short-tempered of late. My restraint was in short supply when the repeated shouts and angry words forced Alasne to tears. I got up, determined to let the old man have it once and for all. She sensed my mood and held up her bandaged hand to prevent me from speaking my mind.

'*No!*' she mouthed, as Menka turned to see who had entered the equipment tent. '*Not yet!*'

He was in a foul state of mind and hacked a great cough before addressing me.

'What do you want, rabbit?' he said. 'Your sweetheart is indisposed, and will remain so to you while I live. Go practise your lute.'

I regained control of my anger. One strike from my toned and hardened fist would end this frail imbecile's life, but Alasne had taught me patience and virtue.

'I will collect and perform with you tonight,' I said. 'Do not touch her.'

'You?' he asked in amazement. 'You know the lines?'

'I've heard them a hundred times,' I replied. 'I also have the first-hand experience of what happens beyond the screen.'

Menka scoffed. 'Do not be late, and attire yourself in something from my wardrobe fitting for the occasion.' He left the tent, and Alasne looked at me with pride.

'Watch out for the mice,' she said. 'Losing one might see us all hanged as witches.'

Fortunately, the act went smoothly, and the troupe was well rewarded for its efforts. I spoke the lines, with one or two grunts of approval from the magician, before taking my place beyond the screen. There was only a slight issue with a fat butcher who misconstrued my attempts to hold him still; he struggled before he turned into a small pig and squealed in astonishment along with the crowd when the screen withdrew.

The coin purse was heavy, and Menka looked pleased but immensely tired. Alasne told me later he had visited and paid for a doctor to see to him, which was rare. He also paid for the doctor to see to her hand, which was unheard of.

Mutual respect developed, and he allowed me to drive his

cart with my beloved alongside. Menka lay beyond in the cart, more and more, as his health and age deteriorated. We often had to cut short our shows due to his lungs, which wheezed and crackled with an incurable malady. The other members of the troupe soothed his ailments to prop up his performances, and the ultimate success of their own. They looked grimly at one another over the evening fire and agreed that it was likely the last time he would make the westerly trip of the Camino. If they were lucky, they might make it back to Santiago itself where there was a new hospital for those who could afford it.

There came a day when we had to decide on our plan for the winter. Should we head to Bilbao and the coast for the longer route to Santiago, which was traditional, or brave the shorter and less lucrative journey back via Logroño? I was growing in popularity, had a healthy dose of good sense and strength of character, and now found myself with the trusted position of deciding while Menka was indisposed.

The magician was too weak to protest about my request for his maps. He jealously guarded them, but as he no longer held the governance of the troupe, I forced the issue and the lock of his strongbox for the parchments. Many black velvet bags of coin lay beneath, but this was not relevant to my search. Menka lay back, relieved I had not come to rob him, but I found one gold coin wrapped into the map. I put it aside, deciding whether to give it to Alasne or return it later; I was no thief.

The faded maps showed many things. They had many unintelligible symbols, dates and markings, likely identifying profitable towns and villages depending on the season. Red and blue inks littered the page, but I made out the spot we were heading for and the crossroads that would take us either north, initially to the coast, or directly west. According to the map, there was a shortcut not far away and directly northeast that I had never travelled. The route would shave a week off our journey north and present us profitably in Santiago in about the same time.

'What is that red cross at the first village?' asked Alasne. 'We've never played there. I'm sure of that.'

'If it was the plague, then we would be fine now. The map is ancient. Perhaps it's just an unpleasant place Menka played in before he met the troupe?'

None of the others had visited or travelled the shortcut, so we agreed to try it. We would play the Christmas markets along the coast, missing out Santander, and get to Santiago to drop off the old magician should he continue to deteriorate. I thought of the gold coins in the chest; they would surely be enough to warrant a comfortable retirement for him.

WE REACHED THE CROSSROADS THE NEXT EVENING AND discovered the track that wound its way through the low foothills of the mountains. I walked in front of Menka's cart like Hannibal leading his troupe of elephants, considering the best commercial option along the route and consulting the map. I balanced my decision to help the old magician, despite his cantankerous nature, with the needs of the other performers. What was non-negotiable was spending the rest of my life with the woman I loved. I resolved to marry and release Alasne from her servitude, whether he liked it or not, by the feast of the Immaculate Conception on December the 8th. I would introduce her to my family and decide on our future together with the money saved from the troupe's split of the season's proceeds.

We passed through the first village and folk came out to greet us, being unused to travelling troubadours. The troupe played a few tunes and taught the children to juggle in exchange for necessary provisions.

We left in a hurry, following an unfortunate outburst from Menka.

He had risen from a coughing fit to find the unfamiliar surroundings, and the route changed from his expectations. His mood soured when I assumed control of the proceedings and challenged his authority.

'I see the rabbit has grown horns while I have been ill,' he said.

'I have grown sense, and we will travel this route for the benefit of all, especially for yours,' I replied with the nodding approval of the others.

'Do not travel further up this road,' he said, 'not unless you wish to face the devil himself!'

The troupe murmured. They were superstitious and still clung to Menka's leadership, despite the scoffs from the villagers that they were God-fearing people in this quiet part of the world. We settled the matter by agreeing not to enter the village marked with the red cross, but Menka covered his wagon and sealed it against the outside world.

'Bloody fools!' came the muffled cry from inside the caravan. 'I'll not come out till we are over the mountains.'

Alasne and I led the horses and caravans out onto the narrow winding path, suffering the slurs and insults from within until he fell asleep and we could hold each other without being seen.

The map was inaccurate with distance, and we arrived at the outskirts of the portentous village before noon. Folk came out to greet us, and we hesitatingly continued, with much thanks for the offer of refreshment. The troupe relaxed and enjoyed the waving crowds, eager to make us stop and hear our news from the lowlands to the south. It reminded me of my village, far away to the east, which grew closer with every horse step.

Menka remained silent throughout the ascent and through the village. Alasne became concerned that he might be ill and unbuttoned the front canvas to check inside. His face was white with fear, and he clutched at his books. We were through the village before we encountered the reason behind the red cross.

A man of immense age blocked the track leading out from the village. He leaned on a tall staff and looked ready to expire at any moment.

'You've come back, then, you old fox,' he said, looking behind me into the caravan. 'Come out and face me, you scoundrel, and give me back what is due!'

'Never,' shrieked Menka. 'Our master promised me the books before he died.'

'Pah,' spat the old man in the road, 'and what have you done with them, eh? "The Most Magnificent Menka", a simple street conjurer of cheap tricks.'

'Walk on, Alasne,' commanded Menka. 'Do as you're told, girl!'

The horse moved, but the old man stood his ground and stared up. 'You watch out, girl, he'll rob you of your future too, just like he did mine. I'm penniless for my trust in him and his promises, but just you wait and see – I've got a few tricks of my own.'

'Don't listen to him. Haven't I always looked after you?' said Menka.

The man held up his staff and pointed it at the caravan in a mock pretence of a powerful wizard.

'You're not long for this world, you old rat,' he said, 'but it won't be my doing that takes your miserable life. Your tricks will unravel, and there will be an end to the old magic. I always had the better second sight of the two of us, even Master Stephano said so.'

Menka shrieked at the sound of his former master's name and buttoned the canvas to end the conversation. I remembered the gold coin in my pocket and tossed it to the old man to let us pass.

'Charity, Master Rabbit?' he said.

I wondered at the coincidence or how he had arrived at the nickname.

'I prefer recompense, in as far as I have the means,' I replied.

'Ah, a kind soul with a long future with the beautiful woman beside you. Thank you for your generosity, but who can say whether you too will unravel? Perhaps not, but the magic will decide whether you and your spirit form are already truly one or not.'

I nodded in respect but concluded nothing from the exchange and the cryptic ramblings of the old man.

We carried on until late afternoon and struck camp in a resinous forest clearing beyond the highest point of the mountain road. Menka regained his strength and temper from a tonic, and the lively exchange earlier in the day. He discovered the charity I had given and the theft of his coin and would not permit me anywhere near his cart, caravan or Alasne. I suffered the humiliation of being transformed without the screen, and here I return to the beginning of my tale.

Menka transformed me into a rabbit for my act of charity, and I was caged for three days.

Alasne cared for me while I endured the punishment, and I returned to my form late in the day, in time for a performance in the first town along the coast. The salty air cleared my head of thoughts of grass and burrowing, and I finally got used to walking upright on two legs, which took over an hour to become reacquainted with.

Menka's mood lifted with the enormous crowd and the thought of rich pickings. Alasne was so pleased to see me returned that she endured the heckles, jeers and offers for sexual encounters from the maritime flotsam and jetsam before the stage. The platform was secure, and the troupe gave me the night to recover from my ordeal, but I watched all the same, at the beautiful woman in stage paint and silken clothes beneath the lamplights of the stone quay.

Menka goaded the mettle of the sailors and townsfolk, some of whom had seen the act before.

'Who among you is the bravest?' he asked. 'Man, woman or child?'

There was much pointing and raising of hands. Alasne lit the candles surrounding the screen and placed Menka's books next to his mystical devices, then assisted the magician with his shaking hands to tie the blindfold around his pale head.

'Turn Gorge into an ass!' one sailor shouted. 'He knocked over the captain's measure of rum, and we were all flogged for it.'

'Do you have the coin?' asked Menka.

'I'll pay!' joked one of his shipmates.

'I'll double it if I can ride him!' called another, reaching for his purse.

The penitent man staggered up the steps and was led by Alasne to the screen. I always had a pang of jealousy and apprehension for her when she was out of sight. Occasionally, there was unlooked-for romantic intent, and she called for help from the strongmen brothers, my closest of friends. The choice of the donkey did not involve her having to embrace the drunken sailor, so I relaxed.

Menka huffed and puffed without his usual enthusiasm. He panted out the incantation and struck the floor, igniting the flash powder, signalling for the screen to be parted. The donkey beyond honked and bellowed its surprise and Alasne guided it around the stage to the astonishment of the crowd. Only I watched in horror as Menka clutched at his chest and staggered, looking for support; something was wrong. The sailors pointed and hollered at the comedy of the old man staggering around like a lunatic, trying to keep up with the girl and the donkey parade. He knocked over several lit oil lamps, spilling their burning contents onto the dry boards. I rushed forwards through the deep crowd, but it was too late, and I saw Menka whirl and fall into the screen. He clutched at the fabric, dragging it down into the open candle flames at its base, as the stroke he was suffering burned his mind.

The fire took hold of the dry canvas rapidly, and the troupe fought their way through the mass of spectators, trying to gain access to the stage. It was all over. Menka's robes caught fire, and he twirled in panic, wreathing himself in flame. He reached out to save the books on the side table, clutching them to his chest. He screamed and burned alongside them as panic ensued in the crowd. The stage caught alight, and I pulled Alasne from the platform, leaving the donkey to rear on its hind legs before taking flight down the cobbled harbour steps and onto the sands of the beach.

A team of sailors, used to the danger of fire, put out the worst using buckets of seawater. We dragged the lifeless form of Menka from the smouldering floorboards, and I prised the partially scorched book from his hands. The leather cover was blistered, and the flames had burned a sizeable chunk of one corner, burning through every page. A final bucket of water doused the smouldering tome and the smoking robes of the magician.

It wasn't until later, while consoling Alasne along the beach, that I noticed the hoofprints and realised the legacy of having no magician, and no means of transforming the animal back into the sailor. In the confusion and panic, his shipmates assumed he had fallen into a drunken stupor after his escape from the back of the stage, and now lay in sublime contentment snoring somewhere along the coast.

He would never return to them, or the form of his birth, though perhaps he had already attained the true spirit assigned to him by the ancient magic. Even as we followed the prints in the sand, the tide was turning and washing away the memory of the man and what had befallen him. We found the animal grazing on the headland, and it staggered comically towards us. Whether this was because of the excessive grog he had consumed, and the last he would ever taste, or whether the option of having four legs needed time to get used to, I could not tell. Alasne was confident that with time and study, we could try to restore the man, and we returned later with the troupe to halter him. He clip-clopped behind us for the rest of the way to Santiago, and Alasne took great care of him.

We paid a hefty fine to the town office for the fire and saw to the burial of Menka. The troupe realised that without the magician, they would need a new headline act.

The solution came by accident when Alasne discovered the sailor-turned-donkey could still comprehend speech. We bargained with the animal to assist us in the show, in exchange for our diligence in unlocking the secrets from the charred book that would return him to his life on the sea and the taverns on land. 'Pedro the Counting Donkey' was a novelty and highly successful act along the coast, only limited by the sailor's inherent difficulty in multiplying numbers together; we stuck to addition and subtraction, and the money bowl was full most nights. Everyone in the troupe gained a share, and a sense of equality and freedom of expression manifested itself in the blossoming of fresh ideas and creative works.

We divided the magician's belongings fairly amongst ourselves, and Alasne took over the horse and caravan. She had owned nothing before, and it took a while before she stopped asking if she could use items that now belonged to her. I took charge of the books and studied the unintelligible writings and diagrams without success; the secrets of the magic had died along with the old magician. Alasne opened the lockbox in front of the troupe and shared out the wealth in the black velvet bags. There were stubborn refusals from our fellowship, and it was finally agreed that she would keep a full third of the gold, making her a wealthy woman.

I proposed to her one evening on stage, in front of a friendly village crowd, and she accepted to great applause. Her caveat was that we would wed after we had returned to find the old man in the village and see what he could do to reverse the poor sailor's condition. Menka's fellow apprentice, under the same master, might shed light on the solution. At the very least, we could return the books and property he had so fervently believed were partly his.

The following spring, we said our goodbyes to the troupe, and I pointed out the village where my parents awaited us; perhaps the troupe would visit to play for us, and Alasne and I would perform a swansong. We returned to the settlement bearing the red cross to discover the old man had passed away several months prior. I buried the remains of the book next to his stony grave, and we broke the news to the donkey.

Despite the attempts to leave the poor beast behind with an honest farmer, the animal followed us back to my family home. There was a tremendous welcome, and I was glad that most of my letters had reached them throughout my wandering. They made a great fuss of Alasne, who had never known the warmth of an actual family.

We married in the village at the end of May, and she invested in the small family farm by buying up orange groves nearby, and several of my old harvesting friends moved back to work for us. I built a home, and on her birthday, I made a stage for Alasne to sit and practise her sleight of hand. It was during a warm evening not long after the harvest that the troupe arrived, slightly diminished in size but better equipped and full of the fortune they had experienced since our departure. It wasn't until we had finished hugging one another and the last caravan had pulled up that I saw the team of six donkeys behind.

'There's something you should know,' said the old carpenter, taking me aside. 'The people Menka turned into animals and back again...'

I glanced at the donkeys and saw the same muted, resigned look of the transformed sailor in their eyes.

'The magic is unravelling, just like the old man in the village said it would?' I said, interpreting his look of concern.

'Yes,' he replied. 'We bump into villagers in the places we used to play. They say husbands and wives are missing, and after we pass through we are followed by donkeys, rabbits, and you name it. We passed through the village of the red cross, and we discovered the same as you did; there is no deliverance for them.'

'You think the magic has decided their spirits do not align with their animal form?'

The old carpenter nodded. 'If they are changing then perhaps... well...' he looked over nervously at Alasne who was laughing with her old friends, 'you might too.'

'How long have I got?' I asked, fearful at the thought of leaving my wife and family.

'The places where we visited and where the beasts show up, we passed through ten years before we met you. I'd say you've got at least that amount of time.'

'The old man said he couldn't be sure of my fate,' I said.

'Perhaps my charity and naivety will see me through. I can't comment on my trustworthiness or innocence.'

'I can,' he said, putting a hand on my shoulder. 'I think you'll be fine. Not everyone Menka turned goes missing; I thought you should know.'

They stayed for a whole fortnight and played many nights in and around the village. People came from miles around to see the act, the seven counting donkeys, and the beautiful woman who performed magical tricks by the sea.

———

I LIE AWAKE LATE INTO THE NIGHT THESE DAYS, LISTENING to her sleeping, and the gentle snoring of our ten-year-old twins in the next room. They have their mother's eyes and my wanderlust spirit. Even now they can make a peseta disappear and reappear as well as any magician I have seen; they play together most days on the stage, and Alasne is teaching them to dance. I wake every morning, clasped by the woman I love, fearing to open my eyes, but comforted that I will always be held no matter the form, by my beloved magician's apprentice.

THE DARK HEART

No one sat in Simkin's chair, ever.

Those who dared to try to sit in his customary place ended up with ears boxed as a painful reminder of his status as the most prolific and wicked bully ever to have disgraced the venerable halls of the King Henry VII School for Boys.

The chair in question afforded a high and noble position within the choir of the school chapel. 'Simkin's Throne', as it became known during his short tenancy of it, was the only seat in the stalls to be closed in on both sides. The chair granted the ill-tempered youth a perfect opportunity to snooze through divinity lessons and church services. He could sleep off his nocturnal villainy safely, knowing that his band of miserable cronies were keeping an eye out. These lesser villains were eager to master the art of cruelty that would one day make them successful bankers, lawyers, and politicians. They thankfully had little of Simkin's evil spirit and followed mostly out of fear, enjoying their immunity to punishment at the unpleasant hand of the son of the Duke of Argyll.

The rogue's pedigree afforded many a blind eye from the

masters. In all his school years, only a mild remonstration had occurred during a bitter incident which led to a newly arrived second former being found unconscious.

The richly and intricately carved stalls in the choir displayed three hundred years of scratches and signatures. Each schoolboy had scrawled his name on part of the medieval chapel, the added graffiti a memento mori for generations of boys to come. It was the curious carvings at the end of the armrests, the pulpits, and the Gothic pelmets that attracted scholars and visitors to the school chapel. These notable works were often pieces carved by apprentices during the Middle Ages, allowing the young craftsman to practise their art before being allowed to work on the more artistic and profound ceiling roses and bosses. Many curious and mythical beasts, laughing monks, knights on horseback, or fiendish gargoyle-like creatures were carved, paving a road to the rank of journeyman carpenter.

Simkin's chair was of altogether darker wood, felled and shipped from the Indian subcontinent, and had two identical creatures on the armrests. They were gryphon-like creatures, winged, with open beaks and piercing eyes. Those who saw them became convinced that the artist must have had access to the beast in life. The figures were worn and smooth, with a polished patina, but the end of their curved beaks and hidden teeth remained remarkably sharp given their great age.

Simkin, when fully awake, hooked and poked his fingers within the unwholesome mouth. He would often deposit his stolen and well-chewed gum within the gaping maw, much to the annoyance of the school porters who had the unenviable task of trying to retrieve the sticky substance.

There was a blessed relief during the holidays when boys could no longer turn up injured, robbed, tormented or tortured. Sanity amongst the staff returned all too briefly when Simkin went home for the few precious weeks. For many of the younger boys, the holidays could not come soon enough. The silent and public tears they shed at the school would emerge once again on the eve of their return, but protestations from them brought no mercy from their dutifully oblivious parents. The school had an excellent reputation for education and discipline, though much of this 'character building' was conducted out of hours, and freely by Simkin and his merciless privy council. Such instructions remained unrecorded on the syllabus, out of sight of the masters, but not out of mind.

IT WAS ALWAYS THE FIRST GENTLE WEEK OF SEPTEMBER when the violence re-established itself with the return of the pupils, and its own 'Lord of the Flies' took his throne at the start of the new term. Each session he grew older, and more potent, with a free and full diary of wickedness to stretch the bounds of cruelty and his inventiveness throughout the coming school year.

A new arrival, before the start of the autumn term, created something of a welcome change and a distraction for Simkin and his subjects. Boys newly arrived were playing cricket on the lower field, or fives against the wall of the nearby sanatorium. Simkin held court on the highest point of a mound overlooking both the wicket and the imposing Tudor mansion of the school. His courtiers, mostly arranged in rank or status, lounged in the afternoon sun and dreamed of Christmas. The high grassy knoll afforded a superior view over the long and sweeping driveway. New boys arrived in shining chauffeur-driven motorcars, accompanied by fathers who had once studied at the school. Simkin surveyed the field of battle from his position on the mound, watching as each expensive vehicle arrived, dropped off their anxious and tearful progeny, and then departed in a hurried cloud of dry Cotswold dust.

It was the spotless white-walled wheels of a Rolls-Royce Silver Ghost that caused the boys to suspend play temporarily. His 'second-in-command' nudged Simkin from his recumbent surveillance of the field and he propped himself up on his elbows to see the latest arrival. Two olive-skinned men in turbans got out of the front and opened the rear doors to aid the exit of an imposing man. Gaining his full height, the dark-skinned adult smoothed the edge of his luxu-rious silk and cotton robes, bandaged around his muscular and impressive torso. A jewelled turban sat crowned upon his glossy black hair, and he beckoned to the child inside to come and meet the rapidly approaching headmaster and senior tutors.

A boy of eight years old alighted and squinted in the English sunlight before greeting the teaching staff. Four white robes met four black robes, stepping around each other like chess pieces, but the boy handled himself formally and graciously, which was surprising given his age. He presented himself as a carbon copy of the man who turned out to be his father. The two of them went inside while the chauffeur and the servant removed and brought in richly decorated trunks and chests from the gleaming car. One man returned and took out a gilded birdcage. There was a cry of a captive bird and Simkin could see, even at that distance, that a white falcon fluttered within the cage. The bird sported a leather hood and was alive with the sound of small silver bells attached to the leather thong at its feet.

Simkin's mind whirled with the possibilities for harm and mischief, and his racism knew no bounds. His close family circle had influenced him, and the Duke of Argyll had made sure his son shared his lack of respect for the 'heathen'.

The Indian boy's name was Salah, and he had recently

arrived in England. The school introduced him the following day, and even Simkin remained awake, scratching at the dark wooden beasts whose heads lay in his palms. Salah was the son of a Kashmiri prince who was a precious and influential ally to the country. The boy spoke perfect English without a hint of an accent. He had a regal bearing, with no sign of condescension or privilege.

Jealousy ignited in Simkin at once, fuelled by his anger at being the second-richest boy at school.

Simkin's status as the son of the Duke was suddenly far less eminent. He felt that there was an air of complacency amongst his targets whenever he stalked or trapped them. The fear that once held sway was still there, but there was something intangible and meaningless now in the petty theft, beatings and emotional stress he inflicted.

Simkin put it down to this popular boy. There was a wholesomeness and nobility that emanated from the young princeling that Simkin could never equal. It brought Salah a fellowship amongst his classmates and admiration from his tutors. He could continue in the private practice of the pagan religion and culture he had been born into, providing he learned the Christian scriptures and attended church cere-monies on the many feast days. Salah excelled in the reading's delivery, watched on by the ever-alert Simkin, who scowled and muttered from his chair in the choir.

This boy was a threat to his authority and the natural order of the school.

Salah was always in company, and he was too risky to engage, so Simkin and his acolytes bided their time. They watched patiently and beheld a brooding tension build inside their wicked leader.

'Will no one rid me of this troublesome boy?' said Simkin, in a pique of violent malice towards an innocent third former. His cohorts understood the allegory and the quotation; they were brutes, but learned ones at that. King Henry II had requested a similar satisfaction from his knights to deal with the most famous of archbishops, Thomas Becket. Now that edict was being offered to his inner circle. One would rise to prominence if one had the guts and the devilish act to knock this young Indian upstart from his perch.

A sturdy deputy and a gangly subordinate were the first to strike. They lacked only their master's intelligence, cunning, and meticulous planning. They had seen the boy exercising his white falcon on the summer evenings after class. Often, several of Salah's friends would watch, beguiled, as he twirled and danced with the lure. The falcon swirled in the air to match his young master's acrobatics on the ground.

The birdcage sat at a distance, unguarded.

There were a multitude of ways it could serve their master, Simkin; perhaps he would keep it, maybe he would frame another boy with its theft. In both cases, this young warrior prince would soon have his wings clipped. The falcon could stay out in the shortening days until it perished in the misty cold that arrived with the waning of September.

The sturdy boy had the bright idea to shorten the odds by removing the watching boys. He scribbled a note, left his covert companion and circled round out of sight like a sheepdog lifting sheep. He approached the small audience from the direction of the school. Several of the boys, fearing assault or theft, made off, but those that remained enjoyed a kindness they had not yet known from one of their oppressors. Naively, they raced off with the note, apparently from their head of house, requesting an earlier-than-planned room inspection in the dormitory. Late-arriving boys would have their exeat privileges removed for one week.

Alone, and seemingly oblivious, Salah continued his training of the falcon, sending it high into the air for a final stoop. With Salah's attention on the circling bird, the crime began.

Simkin's deputy looked over at his hidden companion in the hedge and gave a silent signal to begin the distraction. The accomplice, deep within the rhododendrons, delivered a high-pitched whistle and Salah turned instinctively to discover the location and purpose of the alarm. The noise alerted a master at the window of the common room, who glanced out over the playing field to see the muscular captain of the school rugby team race over to lift the birdcage. There was an almighty screech from the falcon above, and Salah shouted a warning to the thieving sixth former. The boy took no notice and raced away, unaware of the danger hurtling from above. A final cry from the falcon caused the school captain to look up into the downward path of the extended talons of the raptor.

The boy abandoned the birdcage and fought off the bird of prey, but too late to escape serious injury to his face. His blindness, in one eye from the frenzied claws, meant he never played rugby again or became an officer in the army, much to his father's disgrace.

The internal enquiry concluded a verdict of aggravated misadventure, and the injured boy's colourful record at the school did not encourage the school board to dig any deeper. Significant restrictions on the bird's activities resulted, and they assigned Salah a chaperone during future flights.

Simkin lost two of his dependents in that fell swoop. The school captain left not long after his hospital stay. The gangly youth preferred beatings and abuse along with the rest of the lower school, in penance for his actions, but he never laid a hand on any boy or man again.

The following Sunday heralded the first of the autumnal storms, and Simkin sauntered into the chapel with something caught in his eye that had blown in from the dusty courtyard.

He rubbed at the gritty foreign body until his eye reddened and wept. The empty seat of the recently departed school captain stuck out, but not for long. The boys followed Simkin, rank and file, and Salah left them to sit within the unoccupied pew. There was a sharp and deliberate nudge from his right, reminding Salah of his station.

Salah did not heed the warning.

The service began, no longer allowing a chance to eject Salah from his unworthy place amongst Simkin's inner circle.

Simkin was late to the realisation and stared one-eyed in disbelief at Salah. It embarrassed his henchmen to be next to the young trespasser because they could not effect his removal. There was the outside possibility that a boldness existed within the youngster that needed correction. Simkin would extinguish any pretension that equality existed at the school or within the country at large. He squinted across at Salah and saw that he was watching him with his shallow almond eyes.

'*Beware, dark heart, the dark-wood wakes!*'

The whisper came from around his seat, and Simkin shook his head, confused. The liturgy from below continued, and the voice did not speak again. He rubbed at his eye with his handkerchief and got out a slip of paper and a pencil, out of sight of the ever-vigilant school chaplain.

His smirking cohorts passed it along the row until it reached the boy to Salah's right. He dropped the message into the Indian boy's open hymn book. Salah unfolded it but showed no sign of emotion as he viewed the crude coffin-like drawing scrawled within. Beneath the coffin lay a knife with drops of blood issuing from a hand. The word 'cricket' appeared at the bottom.

Service concluded, the boys filed out, and Salah joined the crowd for the final inter-house cricket match of the year. The rain let up, and the wind subsided, allowing the game to progress. Salah was on the field as a strike bowler and picked up a loose cricket ball, tossed onto the field of play by an older boy who smirked and retired to sit high on the mound. Simkin watched knowingly and majestically from on high. Salah positioned the seam carefully between his fingers, pausing only briefly to notice the protruding razor-blade points worked into the stitching. He looked back sadly at the noisy crowd on the mound at his back telling him to get on with it.

Salah was an excellent seam bowler for one so young and was chasing several records for wickets despite his short season on the field. He raced in and pitched the first ball of the over, full and slow.

The facing batsman couldn't believe his fortune as he clattered the ball high for six runs in the mound's direction. Applause broke out across the boundary ropes for the lucky strike, with the eager and rarely acknowledged batsman raising his bat in the air before returning it to his hands. He examined the deeply cut mark that had embedded itself into the linseed-protected willow and shrugged, unable to explain it.

The hapless and unaware catcher high on the mound screamed in pain as the ball sliced into his expectant fingers. Caught but dropped. He held up his bleeding hand in shock and confusion. Simkin hurriedly exchanged the cherry red corker and threw the original back onto the field of play. All eyes followed the bleeding boy racing in the sanatorium's direction, there to stitch the end of his severed middle finger. Salah stood passively and stared back at the instrument of the boy's misfortune. He shook his head before collecting the ball and bowling out the wildly swinging batsman.

FOUNDERS' DAY ARRIVED IN EARLY OCTOBER; AN EVENT richly celebrated in the school calendar, marking the anniversary of the school. The feast and candlelit evensong brightened an entire day absent from Latin conjugations, classics, and other tedious studies. Even Simkin, with his reduced outreach, could endure an hour of readings and sermons from the benefactors and trustees of the school, in exchange for the best meal this side of Christmas. There was no want, and the masters permitted boys to take sweet-rolls or dainties where such vittles remained at the end of the evening.

There would be plunder and days of theft from the lower school to occupy even the most hardened school miscreant, and Simkin and his reduced retinue would re-establish their authority. He felt he deserved it following the bloodied nose he perceived. There was a growing sense amongst his prey that they could beat the predators. Their number was waning, and things had become easier on the boys who suffered. It was high time to put that right.

The candlelit choral event was consistently a highlight, and many boys stopped pretending to sing on such occasions, finding new careers and a love of music sparked into life in the light of the flickering flames. It allowed the boys more freedom, and they entered the chapel in mixed groups rather than the more formal forms and classes of most mornings. It was this informality that may have explained why it came to pass that the rows of the more elite chairs filled with unfamiliar faces. No one dared to sit in Simkin's chair, and he skulked into the row with his pirates and continued to gorge on stolen booty.

It did not become apparent to the boys that Salah had made a purpose of sitting in the otherwise vacant chair, newly vacated by the unfortunate catcher of the cricket ball. Salah sat in proximity to the source of the school's misery, and he stared with dark and unfeeling eyes at the larger boys until they turned their gazes away. It took Simkin time to discover the source of the unusual hush that typically only occurred with the entrance of the masters. He licked his fingers and screwed up the cake papers from within his screened wooden cocoon. It was his closest advisor who coughed and knocked at the wood panel to alert him to the intruder on their sacred territory.

Simkin looked round in disbelief at the brazen foolishness or cheek of the Indian boy who stared piteously back. He would not stand for this boldness, and a willingness to make a stand to his authority in front of his subjects – not against boys he had reigned in terror over for four years. Simkin did not look away. He felt compelled by this bright champion to endure his gaze, reflecting a mirrored image of himself in the shimmering candlelight. He heard a whisper from within the cubicle.

'Beware, darkest of hearts, for the black-wood wakes, and the black-wood takes!'

Simkin finally broke free of the spell and bared his teeth at Salah. With a melancholy glance from the boy, the altercation ended, and joyful song erupted from the stalls. Unnerved by the challenge and late to his feet, Simkin stuffed the balls of sticky paper, with one long finger, into the opening of the creature beneath his hand. He struggled to withdraw it, and a sharp and sudden sting caused him to stifle a scream, inaudible over the rapturous voices of the chapel. He removed his finger and saw profuse bleeding from something sharp within the carving. The trickle began its red tributary from his finger to his trembling palm.

Only one other remained silent. In turmoil and shock, Simkin wrapped his finger in a handkerchief and pressed at it, looking up and into the solemn eyes of the impassive and silent Salah.

LIGHTS OUT WAS A FULL TWO HOURS LATER THAT EVENING, which gave Simkin time for brooding and planning. The bloodied and bandaged finger had been hidden in his blazer pocket for the rest of the evening, but now, in private, the makeshift bandage came off and the finger was inspected. Simkin was pale with the reminder of the pain and the warning that had come from the surrounding chair. It grew and twisted in the remembrance, from a signal into a challenge from the object of his hatred.

His middle finger was unharmed.

He rubbed at the location of the cut, but the skin felt taut and whole. He wiped the dry blood from all around the digit, careful and fearful at first lest he open the severed flesh. He cleaned the finger more aggressively now, with the remaining white of the blood-soaked handkerchief, and was at a loss to discern or explain the lack of injury.

A piercing cry from the clock tower from across the grassy quadrant broke him from his intense examination in the light of his battery torch. The falcon was awake and rasped in sleepless captivity. It sounded like a warning.

It felt like an opportunity.

He shook his lieutenant, who had been busy with pleasant dreams of his future legal career and the men he hoped to hang, and they stole out into the night. Simkin had developed a network of willing and unwilling aids amongst the porters and kitchen staff, fearful of or eager to please the wealthy and influential menace. He had gained several keys to rooms and chambers, not even accessed by those that stole or cut them for him.

Access to poison and the tower were amongst them.

He dragged his sleepy comrade to the gardener's lodge and unlocked the creaking wooden compound gate. An unsecured shed lay within, containing many wonderful or dreadful things. The choice of poisons in the far cupboard was comprehensive, for the school suffered from a variety of tenacious pests.

He knew that cyanide was tasteless and quick. Agatha Christie had taught him that.

He soaked the end of a sponge madeleine and wrapped it in the bloodied handkerchief, collecting the anxious lookout on his way back to the quadrant.

The waning moon hid beneath a passing cloud, and they waited in a dark recess for the housemaster at the door to finish his pipe. Simkin nudged open the wooden door and lightly climbed the dusty spiral staircase, leaving his right-hand man peering through the crack in the open door.

The falcon cried from the chamber above in expectation of another meal or the chance of moonlit flight. When the door opened, and the unfamiliar shadow appeared, the bird shrieked and battered itself in alarm against its gilded cage.

A light appeared in the dormitory opposite, and the sentry below had second thoughts. After a few minutes, a small white figure quietly made its way across the lawn towards him. He hissed up into the spiralling darkness for his leader to be swift.

Simkin did not hear or heed the warning. The squawking of the falcon subdued as he feigned friendship and unwrapped the poison-stained sponge, offering at arm's length the last meal the bird would ever enjoy.

Below, the boy clicked shut the door and locked himself within, fearing discovery from the person approaching. He inserted the key and turned the iron ring as the footsteps on the ancient cobbles ceased. The key stalled in the lock and became impossible to turn any further. He took his hand from it, wondering whether to escape upstairs to a hidden and cowardly place.

The key turned back with a squeak.

There was silence from above. The boy below could hear the breathing of someone on the other side of the door. It finally spoke, in a deep and resonant voice that appeared to be present in the small antechamber of the tower entrance.

'Redeem yourself through silence and leave this place. I await the dark heart in the chapel, there to judge his wickedness. The dark-wood wakes, and the dark-wood takes.'

The footsteps padded in the chapel's direction, and the boy shook with fear. Simkin came bounding down the steps and into the shuddering form of the lookout. The event above had unexpectedly shaken Simkin, but the message relayed to him by his accessory to avian murder caused his confidence and pride to return. He had no choice but to face this heathen in the chapel, there to bloody and bruise until Salah finally yielded that he alone was master after lights out.

The lookout ran back to his shared room and remained quiet throughout his remaining term. Traumatised by what happened next, and mindful of the words from beyond the door, he kept his promise, and his mouth shut.

Redeem yourself through silence.

He became a penitent archdeacon. He returned only once to the school, after his death. He had requested his ashes be scattered at the site of his formative and 'Damascus' conversion.

Simkin did not have a key for the chapel door, and he didn't need one.

The door gave way quietly, and he stepped onto the moonlit tiled floor and looked towards the end of the nave and the choir stalls. A dark figure leaned forwards from his chair, and he caught the outline of Salah's palms resting in his appointed spot. This was a heresy unheard of, and Simkin took out the handkerchief and strode forwards to meet the rising figure in the shadows of the choir screen.

'Your little rebellious streak is now over. See what I have done,' he said, producing a bloodied white feather from the unfurled handkerchief.

'*Dark heart*,' came a deep whisper, from the shadows. '*The dark-wood knows, and waits for you to claim your right and proper place.*'

'I will deal with you first, you heathen filth,' said Simkin. 'I will cool my battered fists in the font—'

A cry of a lonely and tormented bird of prey cut off the threat. It filled the chapel with its resonant and mournful sound.

Simkin spun around, trying to locate the source of the cry which echoed from shadow to shadow throughout the chapel.

Something stirred near the organ gallery and spread its massive wings. Simkin hesitated, unsure of his eyes. He lashed out at the shadow in front of him, hoping to bring the Indian boy to his knees, but he encountered only air. A second cry from the gallery ended in a long and unwavering screech. He saw the white-robed boy turn for the last time at the open door, staring mournfully with his dark eyes, kindled by the silver moon. Salah left the chapel and closed the door.

Simkin heard it lock shut from the outside, and he raced along the nave, fearful of being locked in for the night, with whatever was inside. He was angry at being fooled. The humiliation amongst the school for this trickery might prove the end of his reign. He pulled and beat at the door, but no sound or help came.

The scratching and scraping from above began again as if a mighty bird shuffled on its perch. Simkin backed down the nave, trying to decide what it was. More substantial than an eagle, and much more significant. He could see its eyes, black eyes reflecting the glancing moonbeams, and blinking with emotionless and cold judgement at the prey below.

Simkin ran, thinking to gain the candlestick holders near

the end of the stalls next to his chair. He heard the beast launch itself with a final cry and beat its broad wings. He wrested the monumental brass holder, but it was too late. The beast was upon him.

He backed into his chair, flailing with his arms to ward off the inevitable. His silence came swiftly and only one penitent boy, still awake and shaking beneath tightly pulled bedclothes, heard the scream from the direction of the chapel.

THE CARETAKER FOUND SIMKIN THE FOLLOWING MORNING. He looked only once upon the lacerated form of the boy, mouth stuffed with a cyanide-tainted handkerchief. He ran out of the chapel and rang the school bell, summoning the masters. One had already visited the tower to discover the unfortunate body of the poisoned falcon. There was a connection, but they never found the truth. Silence prevailed, and life went on following the Duke's short but brutal legal case.

No one sat in Simkin's chair after he died. Plenty came to hear about the strange events and see for themselves the added scratches on the backrest and the curious asymmetrical carvings at the end of the chair arms. The left arm showed a fierce griffon-like creature with piercing eyes and a sharp tongue hidden in the recess of its gaping mouth. The right arm showed a similar creature, but the medieval apprentice that had worked on the mouth had tried unsuccessfully to carve a forked tongue.

The overall effect was, and still is to this day, disconcerting. The carving of the dark wooden right arm gives more than an impression of two legs protruding from the sinister mouth of its beastly guardian.

MY FELLOW MAN

I received the package on my sixty-seventh birthday. It included a key to the lockbox containing the one million pounds, just as User 22772 had promised. His promises were also predictions because he had absolute certainty of future events.

The instructions enclosed were comprehensive on how to avoid any unnecessary attention from the tax officials and the police. They concluded with best wishes for my retirement, and for decades of keeping my mouth shut.

I had done the right thing, and it had blown my mind wide open. I had long ago accepted that my faith in User 22772 and the fantastical events were not mere coincidence or whimsy. To have conclusive proof of that in the letter was both sobering and exhilarating.

When the shaking stopped, I'd contact my old partner in crime, if that is what you could call it. James's banter and quips on the entire affair had been a staple for decades, though he hadn't mentioned it for many months, now that his wife Alice was so ill. I couldn't wait to tell them the marvellous news, and how they would share in this strange fortune. The expression on his face would be worth every penny.

I had not revealed my illness and the recent prognosis to James; Alice was already taking up his entire emotional reserve. I didn't have the courage to tell him he would assuredly lose a best friend and possibly a wife in quick succession.

I read the final solitary line, written in an archaic but flowing script:

You played your part, and now I fulfil mine.

FORTY-FIVE YEARS AGO

It was tedious work sifting through the data, and the internship with the stock exchange was not turning out to be eventful or glamorous. That was all to change.

I had graduated with a good degree from the London School of Economics, just as the financial crisis of 2008 had struck, and found myself stranded with countless others searching for gainful employment. Prolonged months of rejection letters had followed until a company offered a menial position reporting on trends and accounts.

James was already there, working in the same role, and I took to his roguish charms. He would lounge idly or come in to sleep for parts of the day, waking to work in frantic bursts of enterprise that fulfilled the minimum necessary quota. James continued in this way, at a senior level, throughout the rest of his career, but I always felt that if only he had applied that remarkable brain more often to that idle body, then he could have ruled (or at least owned) the world.

The partnership was profitable. I had the precise and

meticulous requirements that James's genius lacked; it's probably why I picked up on the 'anomaly' first.

The markets had been bouncing and rebounding at historic lows for much of 2008 before a shaky and erratic recovery had germinated in the following year. My role was to carry out reviews of brokers and companies for 'variance'. This was a performance-related metric that plotted how close buying and selling activities had been to the market trend. Now and again, a bright spark would get noticed by the company for having predicted, or read the signs of, rise and fall accurately enough to have performed above expectations. Most turned out to be one-hit wonders, having guessed the earlier crash or correction before being unable to repeat their amazing luck and returning to obscurity to try again.

There were hundreds of moderately successful gurus that had navigated the market accurately over a brief period, but they always trailed behind it. They were responding to events and were reactionary. The sharper and more astute followed in hours rather than days. They sold close to the highest value of the day and then bought back at the next lowest point, gambling and repeating until they inevitably got it wrong.

No one anticipated market trends this accurately and for so long.

Not until User 22772.

I scrolled back months to the calamitous and cliff-edged line that corresponded with the collapse of Lehman Brothers and the eventual crash in September 2008. The data was clear, User 22772 was always ahead by a few hours, never reacting but predicting.

The market was almost following the broker.

Not only had User 22772 bought and sold at the best time, but they had predicted the crash and cashed in at the peak of the decade-long bull market in early 2007. There was a missing period of activity during the intervening year and a half before the dark days of September 2008. They had purchased stock at the lowest turn of the market weeks later. Volatility at that point made buying and selling unpredictable.

Not for User 22772.

Scrunching up a torn sheet of paper, I struck my snoring colleague, resting from the exertions of the morning walk to the water cooler.

'Lunchtime?' James asked, jolting from slumber.

'I'm getting lunch every day if you can access the user files. I've found a golden goose laying golden eggs,' I replied.

An idea formed, but I needed links to the confidential live data and details of the one who appeared to have perfect economic foresight. Over a long and drunken working lunch, James had revealed that he had once hacked into the United Kingdom Treasury server out of sheer boredom. The immediate need to destroy valuable computer assets and cover his tracks had provided enough excitement when the breach came to light. He had got away with the crime that time, and I was wondering whether he was bored enough to get information on User 22772 to mirror the activity and invest our pooled and modest savings. We might get fired, but we could still track the user remotely, albeit from an unemployable position at home.

James slid over in his roller chair and reviewed the data. I have always enjoyed seeing the 'penny drop' in people's faces, and this moment I will treasure forever.

'That's not a golden goose,' he said. 'That's a bloody time-traveller!'

James was prone to flights of fancy and was a science-fiction nerd. One of my tricks at parties was to abandon a tiresome guest in James's capable hands with the false asser-tion (as far as I was aware) that the philosophies of big-name authors, such as Bradbury or Clarke, fascinated the individual in question. It only took a few moments with James for the party-goer to leave with a desperate excuse, leaving my friend oblivious as to the genuine cause for the hasty retreat. James was intelligent, but not bright in social situations. The trick backfired one evening when the woman chosen as his next target was able to recite Asimov's Three Laws of Robotics. James and Alice married four months later, and I lost a tennis partner.

'There is a more rational explanation, like insider dealing,' I said, rolling my eyes. 'I'm not interested in how they know, just how to get the profile to keep tabs.'

'It's very naughty,' James replied, with more than a hint of being on board. 'How far back does it go before I risk my neck?'

I scrolled left beyond the steep fall on September 29th, and the activity halted several days before the peak.

'From the top,' I said, 'then again at the bottom in early 2009. Since then they've only been 1.4% variant, and that's likely to do with the lag in the reporting software.'

'That would imply they automate the scheme,' James said. 'No one's pushing any buttons on this one.'

James went back to his desk and hacked in as the admin-istrator.

'Looks like a single broker operating through a holding company. They aren't influencing the market because there's a limit of one hundred thousand pounds per transaction to avoid any suspicion of rigging.'

'That still means they are making a colossal amount when you consider they sold high and bought low at the right time,' I replied. 'Can you access User 22772's live data from the exchange?'

'Better than that,' said James with a smirk, 'I can put a tracking code on the user's activities through the portal they used to access it. The automation software I designed will follow their transactions without lifting a finger. We'll be backing horses that always win.'

'We can't include this user in the list of potential bright sparks for obvious reasons,' I said.

It felt like I was opening the door into a grey world where moral objectivity and ethics were optional.

'Agreed,' said James, following without hesitation, and slamming the proverbial door shut behind us.

I ENDED UP BUYING LUNCH FOR THE NEXT TWO MONTHS. Our scheme blossomed, and our pooled investments rose in value. Every transaction that User 22772 made, we followed courtesy of the hidden code and automated software that James had linked to their account.

Hidden, or so we assumed.

I had often wondered who was making these remarkable predictions and profits undetected. After several bottles of wine, James would theorise on our benefactor's foreknowledge, and I would have to endure hypotheses on wormholes, astral projection, and psychic premonition.

'We can't find them without attracting attention?' I asked, interrupting a boring monologue on special relativity, and catching the waitress's eye for the restaurant bill.

James ceased babbling and leaned forwards. 'Do you want a criminal record?' he said. 'I'm keen to learn more too, but...'

'Excuse me, sir,' said the returning waitress, 'the bill has been settled.'

'Settled by whom?' I said, looking around at the empty late-afternoon dining tables.

'A grey-haired gentleman from last week, sir, paid in cash.'

James jolted from his inebriated state and poked a fork in my direction.

'What did I tell you? Bloody time-traveller!'

I rolled my eyes and buried my head in the tablecloth as he continued.

'He knew we would eat here, and what it would cost, down to the penny. Explain that, then.'

'Why do you think it's the goose that's paid?' I said.

The waitress handed me the gentleman's calling card, and it answered the question:

St Michael's Confessional

20:00

22772

I left the departing waitress a tip and passed James the card.

I felt very nervous. Was this an invitation, or a summons?

'What's a confessional?' he asked, slurring his words.

'Something we are both in need of, apparently,' I replied.

———

St Michael's Catholic church was only a scant distance from where I went to school and was in a wretched and dismal state of repair. I thrust open the creaking door and bumped into a smartly dressed man with a curious birthmark, swiftly making for the outside steps. He looked surprised to see anybody at this hour and continued on his way, turning back to check on us occasionally until he was out of sight.

A giant display board inside greeted us. It held a faded home-printed sign appealing for donations to refurbish the dilapidated building. The musty, dingy space was lit by a few candles, even though the late-evening sunbeams still streaked in, reflecting on the dancing dust motes disturbed by the draught.

'What's that smell?' asked James, fiddling with the diverse home-made crafts for sale near the font.

'Incense,' I replied, seeking the confessional.

James had never stepped into a church before, though he would marry Alice in one. I had made him promise that he would not pursue a '*Star Trek*–themed' wedding, for her sake, and he had taken the advice.

I checked my watch and navigated the leaking-roof buckets on the route to the intricately carved structure near the lectern. There was a window opposite, but the worn and dark wood confessional did not reflect or shine from the setting sun upon it. A large and chipped Victorian statue of St Michael was mounted above, in perpetual mortal combat with the devil at his feet. Faded velvet drapes, tattered with age, hung on one side to reveal an empty and confined booth where penitent sinners came to absolve their sins. The cubicle reserved for the priest lay screened by another curtain. There were a few inches of its interior visible from the floor, and James got on all fours to peep underneath.

'No one inside,' he whispered, which I thought odd considering the church was empty. He made to grab the curtain, but something inside me restrained him.

'Please don't disturb that side.'

To my astonishment, James nodded and complied. There was no snarky comment concerning superstition. As if to lighten the mood, he held up his mobile phone.

'No signal,' he said, 'and Mr Time-traveller is late or winding us up. I'm going for a peek outside to look for any sign of that chap from earlier; he looked shifty.'

I nodded, rechecking my watch. James opened the door, letting in a large gust of wind, disrupting the pamphlets on a nearby table. The churning air continued to dissipate along the nave until its faint breath disturbed the drapery of the priest's booth. The bell-tower struck for 8 pm.

Taking one last glance at the empty transept, and confident that James was maintaining a lookout for any foul play, I entered the confined space of the confessional booth and drew the mouldy curtain shut.

It was dark. The few breaks in the worn material illuminated the faint hint of the lattice, and I waited for my eyes to adjust to the new surroundings.

The remote and muffled bell tolled for the eighth time. I squinted through the screen and saw something shift.

I panicked and reached for the curtain.

'Fear not,' said a soft and reassuring, childlike voice. 'I am incapable of causing you harm, but the confessional must remain in darkness.'

I withdrew my hand and peered through the screen, seeking out the features of the shadow. Whoever sat beyond was more substantial than a child.

'Are you User 22772?' I whispered.

'I'm known by many names,' the voice replied, 'but that particular assignation is the identity of my... assistant.'

'The man we saw leaving?' I asked.

'No,' answered the voice, sharply. 'He serves in another role.'

The shadow shifted.

'You and your associate have been performing well from your little scheme,' it said.

'Don't you mean your little scheme?' I replied. 'How the hell do you predict the market?'

The shadow flinched at the colourful expression, and I felt ashamed given the location.

'I do it because I must.' It shifted away from the screen. 'I have taken certain earthly matters into my own hands, and fundraising is one of them.'

'Fundraising?' I remarked. 'For the church? You've generated a small fortune.'

The voice exhaled a lengthy 'Yes.'

I shuffled on the uncomfortable narrow bench, forcing my feet against the kneeling step that most penitents used to confess their sins.

'How did you discover we are tracking you, and where to find us this afternoon?' I asked, breaking the silence.

'It wasn't challenging for my assistant to discover this, though I have little knowledge of the acquisition of coin. Greed is threatening to ruin decades of my work and your future happiness. I am offering you the chance to curtail your activities,' it said. 'As to discovering your whereabouts, I am divinely talented at that.'

I was uncomfortable and wished that I had never heard of funds, markets, or User 22772. The notions of Mafioso or criminal gangs tracking James and me raced through my mind.

'I'm flattered you won't be providing concrete boots and taking me for a swim later,' I said, trying to regain composure. Humour often got me into trouble, but it regularly got me out of it.

'James thinks you are from the future.'

The voice exhaled into a thin laugh.

'We all hail from the past, do we not? Even I,' it said. 'Cease your trading tomorrow, lest you be discovered.'

I was unsure whether this was a threat, but I had the strange certainty that the voice beyond was trying to warn or help me.

'Yes,' it continued, as though guessing my thoughts. 'Trust your instincts and do not be consumed by mortal things. Your friendship will be tested in the years ahead.'

'How so?' I asked.

'In a distant time, he will need your support and mine,' said the voice. 'I ask you to avoid upsetting my scheme, and I promise to provide for you at the end of your working lives when your needs will be greatest.'

'We are comfortable for years,' I said, musing to the child-like stranger in the darkness. 'I want something more constructive in my life, maybe writing or charitable work. James won't see it that way, though; he is not likely to believe what I have heard.'

I reached for the curtain.

'*No!*' commanded the voice. I retracted my hand as if it had stung me, and it went on gently. 'You have faith that what I am telling you is for the best. Your friend has the same faith in you and the decision you will make for him, though he doesn't realise it yet; he looks to you for guidance – did you know that?'

The revelation in the words struck me.

'He'll be mad,' I said, wavering with my decision.

'For a brief while,' said the voice, understanding my dilemma. 'What follows will make him glad, very glad.'

The shadow shifted.

'My time is brief, despite evidence to the contrary.'

'I will do as you ask, but I have so many questions,' I said, sensing the meeting was coming to a close.

'If you had to ask one question,' said the voice, sounding older and weary, 'one that I would honour to answer truthfully, what would it be?'

I thought hard. So many questions. What did it mean by providing for us? What need would we both face? Why would my decision to end the tracking code and retrieve our investment make us glad? Who or what was in the shadow opposite, pretending to speak with the voice of a child?

The question welled up from somewhere deep inside me.

'Why am I here?' I asked, hoping for a less-than-cryptic answer.

The shadow shifted, and a chuckle came from the darkness.

'The same reason I exist,' it said, 'to serve.'

There was a sudden radiance from beyond the screen, and I shielded my eyes from the piercing light. I was blinded, but I heard the church door open. James called out from the entrance to check if I was all right.

'Whom?' I asked.

'Your fellow man,' said the voice, deeper and more resonant. 'You'll know what to do tomorrow. You will recognise the right time.'

James was running on the tiles towards the confessional, calling out in alarm. He could see the light streaming out from both booths and the heavy curtains glowing in a brooding scarlet.

I gripped the screen and pressed my face against it, bathing in the intense light and trying to make out the figure. My squinting eyes struggled with the effort, but I caught a hint of a majestic form, beaming back.

James ripped the curtain from its rings and dragged me to the hard floor. I saw the dazzling light opposite disappear in a final tremendous flash that unsettled and moved the drawn drapes.

'What the blazes was that all about?' he said, dragging me away from the booth. 'Why didn't you answer me?'

I got to my feet and twisted to face the confessional, just as the sun sank below the level of the window. I reached out my hand and pulled back the priest's drape to reveal an empty booth.

James was bewildered. 'I saw your phone light strobing, and it worried me when you didn't answer. I thought our friend had snuck in and was up to mischief in there.' He glanced into the empty confessional. 'Why did you take a photo of an empty box?'

'I didn't take a photo,' I said. 'Did you see the light?'

'Yes, but what's this all about? Our golden goose hasn't materialised, and you look like you've seen a ghost.'

'No one came in or out?'

'No one,' James replied. 'I had the door open, keeping an eye on the confessional all the time. That shifty fellow hasn't been back either.'

I grabbed James's arm again, and he understood the sincerity and urgency in my voice.

'Let's get out of here,' I said. 'I've got plenty to explain.'

JAMES SAT RUMINATING, SIPPING HIS GIN AND TONIC AT THE quiet, mid-week bar while I related my time in the confessional. I left out that James would need my support; I wasn't sure that telling him of misfortune in our future was the best thing to do.

'Teleportation,' said James, 'or at least some kind of portal. I wished you'd asked him about it, or that I'd ripped off the other curtain first. I could have gone with him.'

I leaned back and rubbed my tired eyes in resignation.

'It wasn't from the future,' I said. 'It was someone or something far older.'

'What?' said James. 'Don't tell me you've gone all religious, not when you are asking me to throw away a dead cert such as we have.'

He folded his arms like a spoiled child, which I presume he had been.

'Hogwash,' he went on. 'They used special effects or something to scare us away; likely that chap we saw running away. I wager they are in there right now removing the speakers and the flashbulb, having a splendid laugh at the simpleton city boys. Haven't you seen *The Wizard of Oz* for God's sake?'

'We will bring ourselves down and attract attention to User 22772 if we carry on. What I don't understand, however, is how I'm supposed to know what to do when the time comes?'

'No idea and I'm too tired to care,' said James. He yawned like a lion. 'Let's talk about it in the morning.'

My sleep was fitful. Circular and unsolvable reasonings filled my mind. I had resolved, despite James's opposition, to fulfil my commitment, and I would need James's unwitting help that morning, plus a diversion.

We met at the coffee shop before work. James broke the awkward silence with his usual and humorous banter.

'Any more angels visit you last night?' he said, stirring his cappuccino.

'No,' I said, ready for the inevitable punchline; James had also had a sleepless night to think of one.

'Shame,' he said. 'I'd love to have had your opportunity, only I'm not a virgin.'

I spat out my tea to see the deadpan face of the man I most loved in the entire world, staring back.

'Bravo!' I said, between violent, lung-filled coughs, and regained my composure.

'What?' said James. 'No comeback? No retaliation? You are up to something.'

After our morning meeting, James and I returned to our shared office and began our 'extra-curricular' routine. He would hack in as the administrator from his terminal to check our investment fund and the performance of User 22772. I would make certain all of our security precautions were in place. I noted frequent foot traffic and bustle in the corridor outside, and any moment the door could open. We both readied ourselves to look busy in our day jobs. The chief's door held the monopoly on knocking.

James whistled as our 'piggy-back' log came through, all courtesy of User 22772 and their activity from the past twenty-four hours. Our automated transactions scrolled on the screen, revealing the total value of our investments. He left his chair and opened the window, stretching his arms in victory.

'Greed is good!' he exclaimed, quoting his favourite line from *Wall Street* to the pigeons on the outside sill. 'Twenty-two thousand pounds, in only twenty-four hours!'

He rubbed his hands and spun around. 'And you wanted to stop because a voice in a box told you to. You're insane.'

I had just logged out when the door opened and the chief crooked his finger for James to go with him. Several unfamiliar and official-looking men stood in the corridor.

'Can you do without Sleeping Beauty here for ten minutes?' he asked. 'I need James to escort these gentlemen around the place.'

'Bring him back when he starts talking about *Doctor Who*,' I said.

James pulled a face and followed the boss out, shutting the door behind him.

The opening and closing caused the wind to blow in through the window, and I got up to shut it, noticing a single white feather on the windowsill. It didn't look like it belonged to the mating birds, scuffling on the edge outside, and the words came flooding back to me.

You'll know what to do tomorrow. You will recognise the right time.

Seizing the opportunity, I typed into James's terminal, withdrawing two hundred and eighty thousand pounds into an offshore account. I navigated to the complex page that contained our software and clicked on the delete command.

'Goodbye, easy life,' I said, and hit the enter key, purging the computer of any trace.

It was over an hour before James returned, ready for a nap. My down-turned face gave the game away, and I braced for the fallout. I had deceived my best friend, and it hurt.

'You've done it, haven't you?' he grumbled. 'You've spoiled the best thing we've ever had.'

I nodded into my hands. He sat down, vexed, and typed laboriously with a single finger into his terminal to discover his precious code was unrecoverable.

'Where's the fund?' he asked.

'In the Cayman Islands account,' I replied, not daring to glance over at my fuming companion.

He worked for several minutes in silence, before grunting with a resigned satisfaction.

'You've covered our tracks,' he said, 'and we've made tenfold on our original stake.'

'Two hundred and fifty thousand in two months,' I said. 'I'm sorry, James...'

He held up his hand as if to deflect my attempt at remorse.

We toiled on, ignoring each other for another ten minutes until it became intolerable. Even when James slept, he snored. He did not sleep throughout that day, and I tried to kick-start a neutral conversation.

'Who were the suits?' I asked.

James glanced over and shrugged.

'No one knows, except that they have come through the parent company; they will be back in the morning. The chief asked me to sound them out, but they were tight-lipped.'

'You think the company is being sold?' I said.

'Maybe. They seemed like the regulatory type,' he said. 'My money is on them being from the Competition Commission or Revenue and Customs.'

I nodded, looking for a way to extend the conversation. James understood my pathetic attempt and continued; I felt forgiveness was not far away.

'Yep, I took them in the lift, and they didn't even break into a smile when I told them the one about the nun and the packet of biscuits,' he said, deadpan as ever.

I often never know if James is telling the truth. It was a very saucy joke, and the thought of my best friend joking inappropriately with strangers in a confined space lifted my spirits, and I burst out laughing.

'You never did!' I said.

James nodded. 'You can ask Janice from accounts; she was in the lift and turned a delicate shade of crimson.'

———

The following day, I was overjoyed to see James at the coffee shop. He had every right to avoid our morning get-together, and I was glad when he spoke first.

'About yesterday,' he said, 'I'm sorry if I came across as an idiot, but we were in this together as partners, you know?'

'Yes,' I said. 'I'm sorry for having gone solo on this. My heart was talking and not my head.'

He slapped me on the back.

'At least I'll be able to have a decent honeymoon and put down a deposit on that flat Alice has been harping on about. It was your idea after all, and I suppose I should be glad I have something out of it.'

I smiled, and we were back to normal.

'Just promise one thing?' James said, paying for my drink for the first time. 'Don't become a monk or something.'

'I might just become a writer,' I said, surprising myself with the outburst.

'Well, don't write about this,' he said. 'Wait until we are old and grey.'

Back in the office, we began our morning ritual out of habit. I caught James trying to log in without realising there was no point.

He noted the quizzical expression on my face. 'Just saying hello and goodbye to our golden goose.'

He frowned and pulled his chair closer to the screen.

'This is strange,' he said, grabbing my attention. 'User 22772 has withdrawn all of their funds. Their portfolio is empty, and they have somehow deleted their activity log.'

'Looks like they cashed in,' I said. 'What time did they do that?'

James typed in a few commands.

'Just after you closed ours – 9.59 am yesterday. Maybe they were following us for a change. Why would they have done that?'

'No idea,' I said, 'but that means we wouldn't have had any golden eggs this morning. Do you think there's another tumble in the markets coming?'

'Maybe,' said James, 'but they never deleted their activity log before. It's like they've never existed, or us for that matter.'

'Well, you can think about it on our way to the morning meeting. It's target revisions today, and we'd better get a move on.'

'I'll meet you there,' said James. 'I need to close this down first.'

I entered the crowded meeting room. Most of the building was there, including the official-looking men from yesterday's impromptu walkabout. The chief paced about the floor.

James appeared and nudged me. 'It's an inspection, a full-blown nook and cranny audit,' he whispered. 'Phyllis from human resources told me just now.'

I was about to reply when the chief coughed and began.

'Guys, I would like to introduce the gentlemen to my right who will carry out an audit on the company's transactional activities and financial health.'

The room filled with palpable tension and fear. Guilty consciences were in for a shock; auditors always sniffed out the faintest whiff of malpractice.

'You will give them your undivided support and help.'

James was shaking, and he glanced over at me, wide-eyed with horror.

'The broker teams will cease any further monitoring and supply all transactional data to these gentlemen on the conclusion of this meeting,' said the chief. The lead auditor leaned over and whispered in his ear.

The chief continued.

'... from 10 am yesterday morning, if you please.'

He moved on to inform the other departments of their compliance, but I didn't hear any of it. My mind was reeling, knowing that I had executed my plan in the nick of time the day before. It appeared the foresighted User 22772 had also pulled the plug at the last moment.

I sensed the penny drop in James. He exhaled and relaxed into a whisper.

'I will kiss you when we get back to the office...'

───────

JAMES TRIED TO FULFIL HIS THREAT, BUT I BEAT HIM BACK with a staple gun.

'I can't bloody believe it!' he said, thumping the desk. 'Promise me you'll listen to your heart more often?'

I smirked.

'You're glad, then?' I said.

'Very glad,' he replied. 'We would have been out on our arses with our assets frozen. You might have gone to prison.'

I took the bait.

'Me?' I said. 'What about the computer genius that put the tracking and automation together?'

'I trust you would have remained silent about that; I am your friend, after all.'

The door opened, startling us. It was the chief.

'Someone's birthday?' he said, bemused. 'Sounds like someone is celebrating. I'd keep it down if I were you. I don't want our guests thinking I'm running a holiday camp.'

James returned to his desk and pretended to work.

'James, I need the data from your two terminals now, from 10 am yesterday, if you please.'

The chief glanced over at me.

'Can I have a word?'

I'd rarely been in his office, and he usually reserved the honour for almighty tongue-lashings. I sat down with some apprehension.

'How long have you been with us?' he said, chit-chatting.

'Two years,' I replied.

'I've been in this business nigh on twenty years, yet I'm often surprised.'

'You mean by the audit?'

'Yes and no,' he said, fiddling with a quilled pen. The feather was white and thick. 'I mean what individuals can get up to from their terminals when they are supposed to be working.'

I struggled to maintain eye contact.

'From terminals like yours and James's.'

I had the uncomfortable feeling that a reprimand was imminent and that I would soon return to the office to box up my things before looking for a new job.

He opened the drawer and took out a letter. I felt crushed. He knew what we had done.

I composed myself and gathered as much dignity as I could. A fluttering of pigeons outside startled me for a moment, and I wavered in my response.

'If I've done anything against—'

The chief interrupted, lifting and pointing the white-feathered quill at me.

'Why are you here?' he said.

The question floored me. Did he mean my role in the company?

I looked at the feather, and the answer came without further hesitation.

'To serve,' I said.

'Whom do you serve?' he asked.

'My fellow man.'

The chief put down the quill. The tension cleared, and he got up to open the window.

'It was you in the confessional?' I said.

He turned and grinned like a Cheshire cat. 'No. I paid for the restaurant, though.'

'You've been following us?'

'I'd say that you have been following me.'

He drew an accurate zigzag line of the market crash with his finger in the condensation on the glass.

'You are User 22772!' I said.

'One of many, but in the instance you are referring to, yes.'

'Who or what was it that warned me to stop trading?' I asked.

'I wish I knew for certain and our mutual friend is always evasive on the subject, but I trust my instinct as you are doing.'

'What happens now, for me, I mean?'

He handed me the letter from the desk. 'This remains between us for the time being, agreed?'

I nodded and scanned the letter. The company would merge, and there would be redundancies whatever the outcome of the audit. The chief's name appeared at the top of a lengthy list of names, ready for termination letters. James and I were not on it.

'I need to make one further addition to the list, and we won't need both of you when we incorporate,' he said.

It sounded like a judgement. 'Are you asking me to choose?'

The chief did not answer and handed me a business card from his top pocket.

'The strangest thing happened yesterday,' he began. 'A publishing house for a charity approached me looking for a ghostwriter on economic matters, and they seemed willing to provide a decent advance for someone I could recommend.'

Our mutual acquaintance had thought of everything.

'If I leave,' I said, 'it would be for James, not for that. He must remain ignorant about my choice.'

The chief nodded and got up to show me out. He offered me his hand, and I took it.

'Good luck with your writing,' he said.

'Good luck in your future fundraising,' I replied.

THE PRESENT

I made my mind up to visit the lockbox first and call James and Alice later in the day once I had processed everything. My hands still shook from opening the letter, but also from the side-effects of the potent retroviral drugs keeping me alive. I had assumed it was a joke, but even James, at his worst, would not have conceived this level of cruelty. I had based my life as a successful writer and charity campaigner on those few minutes in the confessional. The only other who knew about the visitation was the chief who had passed away at a ripe old age. He could have sent it or had someone else arrange it, but my thoughts returned to the bright radiance.

As to discovering your whereabouts, I am divinely talented at that.

I picked up my silver-topped walking cane, a retirement gift from James, and took the key and the bus to the central London address provided in the letter. I knocked, and a doorman took my calling card and ushered me in. The domed lobby was opulent with Italian marble, and many pillared corridors led away to other distant chambers. The doorman walked me to a small vestibule and introduced me to a clerk sitting behind a black mahogany desk. He glanced down at my credentials, and then at my cane in astonishment.

'We've been expecting you,' he said, 'for a very long time.'

'Forgive me. I only received the letter this morning,' I replied.

He seemed even more surprised.

'Well, box 22772 has been waiting for you and your associate for...' He looked at his holographic screen before continuing. 'Forty-five years, three months and sixteen days, to be exact.'

'The box has been waiting and locked for that length of time?' I asked.

'Yes,' he replied, 'and the description of your cane and personal appearance is beyond doubt. We shall dispense with the security arrangements if you can answer the question set in the sealed envelope I have in my custody.'

I waited as the clerk left the room and returned with a

faded and time-worn letter. He looked puzzled on reading the contents but fulfilled his duty.

'Whom have you served?' he asked.

My voice quavered as I thought on memories deep and buried.

'My fellow man.'

The clerk appeared satisfied and extended his arm. 'This way. The other gentleman awaits you.'

'Other gentleman?' I asked as he led me down the stairs and through a bio-security terminal.

'If you please,' he said, pointing to a door with an armed guard.

I went in, and the door closed behind me. A tall and crooked figure sat inside, next to a small conveyor belt which linked to the impenetrable vault beyond.

'Why the hell didn't you tell me you were sick?' said James, waving a piece of paper in front of me.

'You got a letter too?' I said, deflecting the question.

'Too bloody right,' he said. 'There are plenty of other secrets in there too. Does redundancy forty-odd years ago ring any bells? You fell on your sword for me, and you said nothing.'

'Why would I?' I said, embracing him. 'You are my friend and fellow man.'

James squeezed me hard.

'You damn fool,' he said. 'This on top of Alice's illness.'

The conveyor belt started, and we both turned to study the small opening at the far end of the room, like tourists waiting to collect holiday luggage.

'It will be all right,' I said. 'I have received a million new pounds if my letter is true. Alice will be able to get that treatment in the States now, do you understand?' I held up the key to lend weight to my argument.

'I don't want your bloody charity. You'll need it for yourself if our Mr Magwitch is telling the truth about your condition,' he said, waving his letter again and referencing the mysterious benefactor from Dickens' *Great Expectations*. His old and crooked fingers lifted out a key, which he stuck in my face. 'I got this in my letter, and the same amount.'

There was a brief rattling sound as the object made its arrival through the hatch and stopped in front of us. It was large, metallic and about the size of a shoebox, with two keyholes.

'Will you look at that!' said James, squinting at the lustrous top.

Something was etched into the lid, and I got out my glasses. A fine zigzagging line trended up and down. James laughed and pointed at the peak.

'It's the crash of 2008,' I said, 'in perfect detail, as far as I can remember.'

'It even stops where you pulled the plug,' said James.

I pushed my key forwards into the bottom lock, wondering if it was the right one. There was a click as the mechanism engaged part way.

James hesitated. 'Whatever is in there,' he said, 'I want you to know I'd trade it all for your years of friendship.'

I nodded in silence as he inserted his key and opened the box.

The lid rose, and I swear there was a faint hint of incense. Inside was a cloth-wrapped package with James's name on it. Attached were two strips of paper containing numbers and sort codes for us to receive the windfall. I considered how little one million old pounds would have been worth now with inflation. What I couldn't understand was how our benefactor could have known about the currency change only a few years prior when they deposited the box over forty years ago.

James lifted out and unwrapped the bundle. A decorated

leather-bound book lay within. He opened the cover and snorted.

'*The Time Machine*, by H. G. Wells,' he said. 'Someone's having a laugh, because it's a fake. The paper is as white as if they printed it yesterday, though the signature looks genuine enough.'

He handed me the book, and I looked at the imprint. It was the first edition, and the author's pen was sharp and fresh. The paper was pristine, but when I closed it again, the aged and brown patina from the collective page edges was visible. The book had lain closed for over a century.

'You aren't thinking in four dimensions,' I said, showing him the evidence of its antiquity. 'You won't be able to sell it, but maybe that's the point.'

James took back the book and held it until he had made his mind up.

'A gift from the past and the future,' he said, looking inside the box. 'There's something else in here; it must be for you.'

I peered in to see a large swan's feather, resting above a gold-embossed calling card. It held my initials on one side and an invitation on the other.

St Michael's Confessional

20:00

'What does it say?' James asked.

'It's blank,' I lied. 'I'll explain about the feather another time. Let's sort these payments out and tell Alice the marvellous news.'

James closed the lid of the box. 'Then you will tell me all about your situation,' he said, with strained concern. 'Whatever it is, we'll get through it together.'

I offloaded my worries and anxieties about my fate later that afternoon. I had not expected it to be so cathartic, and the unburdening of my soul released like a pressure valve.

James left me, convinced I had told him everything, with the promise that we would spend our collective fortune on treatments that would cure Alice and prolong my life, and our friendship.

I paid my respects to the chief in the graveyard adjoining St Michael's, wondering what part he had played or arranged in the day's remarkable events. His final resting place was no coincidence, and while I had visited the church and the confessional countless times, the experience had never recurred.

Until now.

I entered the restored sanctuary through the glass screens holographically displaying the Victorian door. The old wooden doors were removed during the restoration and replaced with the emergent technology of the time. Inside was empty, and in magnificent condition, but the sanctuary still held on to its original atmosphere. I swung my cane on the tiles and click-clacked my way to the confessional, surrounded on both sides by virtual candles.

I noted the cross-stitched drawn curtain on one side as I entered the connecting booth. My heart raced with nervous expectation as I pulled the luxurious drape across and waited for the tower to strike at 8 pm.

The last bell sounded, and a soft radiance filled the adjoining cubicle, illuminating the lattice from behind.

'Are you ready to serve again?' said the childlike voice, excited as though addressing a friend long missed.

I pushed my face closer to the screen.

'Yes, but it's my time that grows short on this occasion,' I said. 'You know about my illness?'

'Let me worry about that,' it said. 'There is much to do for your fellow men, and I need your assistance for a long time.'

FAMILIAR'S END

The metal detector screeched in Cameron's headset, and he stopped to investigate the promising spot. He dug, and tossed aside an exposed piece of industrial slag before returning to hunt for something of greater interest.

It had been an unprofitable, and misty, morning along the wide cattle-grazed avenue. Still, the weather promised to improve for the last afternoon of his holiday, so he continued on, setting the mayflies dancing from his measured gait through the damp meadow.

Cameron passed the detector back and forth, advancing methodically through the longer grass, surprising an early fox. He made for a slight rise in the ground, just off centre along the wide and ancient elm tree avenue that had once been the great entrance to a long-ruined manor house. Only outbuildings and stables now survived, nestled in the valley hidden in the mist. He searched for the thin disc of the sun above and rubbed his aching neck. A brief sunbeam broke through into the pleasant and fragrant May morning, and the small windows of the church became gilded with the golden rays. It would be interesting to peek inside when he had accomplished the hectare; he liked old things but had discovered nothing better than a Georgian penny this past week. The distant figure of a man observed him from the low church-yard wall, shielding his eyes from the ray of sunlight.

He wandered on, sweeping his detector, unable to shake off the sense of being watched, though he was conscious of the unpleasant feeling long before he had noticed the figure up above. An uneasy sensation had been with him most of the morning but was prevalent here at the woodland edge. His imagination had gotten the better of him when he thought he had heard growling as if a beast were warning a rival. He had shaken off the notion as mere fantasy but had left one ear-piece free. The idea was sapping his enjoyment, so he moved away to a more open area of ground, and the feeling subsided. Mist obscured the trees once more from his view.

The avenue marked a long, broad cutting through the forest linking the church above with the tiny village and its pool below. Cameron's landlady at Long Ride Bed & Break-fast informed him the wide-open space was a hunting ride, once attached to the ruined manor house nearby. It was common land, and Cameron was free to prospect there, provided he followed the correct etiquette and avoided the cattle. Folk didn't spend much time on the rough grass, preferring to take the longer and more meandering route via the lane. There were hints about 'terrible luck and supersti-tion', though the new owner of the hostelry was not a native to the area. She considered the lack of interest in the avenue less to do with ill omens and more because of cow pats and marshy ground.

'Watch out for Jenkins, the churchwarden,' she had said, 'often up at the church, watching over the avenue in all weathers. Though what he has to watch out for, he doesn't say to newcomers like me.'

Cameron turned to look ahead, and the figure was still there, studying him.

A movement in the mist in front of the opposing mass of trees caught Cameron's attention, and he froze, trying to assimilate the cursory glimpses. The white noise in his headset burst into life, and something else came whispering through that caused him to start.

'Here... link them together...'

It was a child's voice, repeating itself more insistently each time. Cameron raised his headphones to verify if the sound was coming from the outside world or his sensitive apparatus. The equipment did occasionally pick up distorted human chatter, either through a buried cable or pirate radio, but this was clearer. The voice returned louder and sharper when he replaced the sweaty headset, damp with dew.

'Here, link them together!' said the voice, almost upon him on his left. The static died down to a murmur.

He caught sight of a girl at the edge of the mist, some way from the margin of the trees. She was wearing a short smock with a heavily stained front and was pointing down to a nettle-infested patch of ground.

Cameron called out, but there was no reply. He turned up the gain dial on his detector, and the static returned. When he glanced back to the rise, there was no one there.

He made his way through a patch of dense nettles to the area beyond where the child had stood, and tripped on a block of stone emerging from the long grass like a rocky iceberg. Once cleared of undergrowth and muck, Cameron discovered a deep socket at its centre. He pushed his small spade down into the central hole, and the tool slid down without effort. It was an old marker post, he thought, and he passed the detector over the spot to reveal only background noise. He moved a few feet away and prospected once again.

His headset screeched loudly, and the adrenaline-fuelled

excitement of a positive find took hold. He isolated the location like a dog sniffing and searching for its favourite ball. The signal was so intense that he altered the sensitivity and turned down the volume. Glancing down at the instrument cluster display, he expected the likelihood of iron. Not gold, silver or any hoard, then; just a buried agricultural relic. The sense of watchfulness from the woodland edge became tangible, and he looked up, conflicted with signals from his instinct and his metal detector.

Sweeping the ground with the detector one last time, he drew out his foldable spade and unearthed the spot. He occasionally paused to pass the head of the machine over the spoil and monitored the woodland margin for any repeat of the uneasy dread.

Negative.

He dug down into the stony earth, and a few inches later he struck a rusty crust; what lay beneath was close. Delicately scraping away the deposit in the pale chalky soil, he pulled out a metal ring, two inches long and matted at one end with fibrous hair. The elongated link had a thin parting as though it had once been part of a massive chain. Cameron pulled aside the hair and took out a cloth to rub the soil and rust from its dull surface; an unremarkable bit of iron, but on closer inspection, something with a thin engraving:

'Rose'.

Cameron examined the find, which was heavy for its size, before stowing the item in his backpack for a more detailed examination back in his room. He checked the hole for any further finds before backing away, one eye on the inky silhouette of the nearby trees.

A rustling movement from within caused him to panic, and he called out.

The girlish voice reappeared in his headset.

'Run... Hide!'

Dread returned, and he scanned about, trying to locate the sizeable four-legged shape encircling him in the mist. The growling was unmistakable, even without his headset, and the wolf-like beast emerged and advanced towards him. A smell of dank, overpowering stagnant water caused him to gag, and the air became saturated with moisture. There was to be no calling out on this occasion, and he dashed in the church's direction, his valuable equipment swinging and jangling at his side, making full flight impossible. He turned to discover that the grass beyond was being parted by something, insubstantial and at a distance, but closing rapidly. A warning cry came from the figure at the church.

'Over here! Hurry!' the man yelled, dashing forwards and wielding a baseball bat in readiness for what followed.

Cameron didn't need any further incentive. Something nasty was not far behind, and he looked back once more to catch sight of the four-legged creature. It was blurred, as though perceived through water, but there were teeth, and it was gaining on him.

'Drop it, man! Leave the damn stuff!' the man ahead shouted.

Cameron abandoned his pack and his detector before vaulting over the low dry-stone wall of the churchyard. He rushed at the iron ring of the massive church door, hearing a snarl from his pursuer, and obscenities from the man swinging his bat to drive the creature back to the lychgate.

'Get the door open, quick!' shouted the man, thrashing at the mist's edge.

Cameron fumbled with the worn latch, rattling and forcing it skyward to disengage the mechanism. The man came sprinting back and flung himself against the door, just as the latch lifted, and they both fell into the dim interior.

They stumbled to their feet, and Cameron heard the man cry out in pain as he clutched his ankle. He slammed the door shut, and thrust his back against the Georgian oak, listening to the thing tearing at the timber from the porch. The other man limped over to aid him in pulling down the handle and throwing both door bolts for good measure. Now that the door was firm, Cameron crouched down to peer through the keyhole. Insubstantial and lidless, a bloodshot eye stared back; its narrow slit of a pupil, like that of a wild goat, opened and closed like a bellows. Cameron could see the lychgate through its spectral form, and he recoiled in horror to reinforce the man with his back against the door. A howl of anguish came from beyond, accompanied by a renewed scraping as the thing tried to gain entry to the sanctuary.

'Don't worry,' said the man. 'We're safe in here now, and I'm the one it wants, likely enough.'

The beast gave a last whimper of anguish before padding away over the dry-stone wall and disrupting the coping stones. They listened as it encircled the church, howling below the windows and shuffling through the gravel of the path. There was a definite limp to its gait now that it was walking rather than running, and Cameron wondered if the old man had connected bat with bone during his heroic sortie from the wall.

'What the devil is that?' Cameron demanded of the grey-haired man, whose fingers were white from the intense grip on the bat.

'Just that, more or less, and something that has been haunting this village for generations,' he replied, panting heavily. 'I've never seen the damn thing that close before; Christ, it's enormous.' His manner changed from panic to one of exasperation.

'Weren't you warned not to go fooling about on the ride?' he said. 'Especially today.'

'The woman at the B&B mentioned some nonsense about witchcraft and such...'

The man threw down the bat in disgust, and the sound of the wood hitting the tiles echoed within the empty white-washed building. He leaned over to rub at his ankle.

'She's a newcomer and thinks we are all superstitious twits. Lucky for you I was here; I was about to call it safe for another year till you started digging about.'

Cameron peeped through the keyhole again. He remained for several minutes in the awkward crouch before easing into an upright position; there was no sign of the thing.

He removed his coat and shivered as the warm sweat met the cool cloistered air.

The man relaxed now that the immediate danger had passed and held out his hand by way of introduction. 'We will be here a while; the name's Jenkins.'

Cameron shook his hand and introduced himself as loose stones tumbled from the low wall outside.

'What is it?' he asked again. 'An escaped wolf? It's huge, but not altogether solid when you look at it.'

'Not a wolf, lad,' replied the man. 'Something far nastier – closer to a fox but much bigger. I wish you hadn't disturbed the creature.'

'I've disturbed nothing,' he said. 'It was already in the wood before I noticed the girl.'

Jenkins pricked his ears with the mention of the child.

'About eight years old, short white smock?' he asked.

'Yes,' said Cameron, patting his coat for his mobile phone. 'We need to call the police or whoever; she'll get bitten or worse if that thing finds her.'

'The thing can't hurt her, not anymore,' replied Jenkins. 'No point in the police. It will just flee back to the wood and disappear for another year.' He gripped Cameron's arm. 'Are you going to tell them a centuries-old witch's familiar is prowling outside St Thomas'?'

Cameron discontinued his search; the phone was in his

pack several hundred metres away on the damp grass. 'Don't be daft,' he said, speculating if the landlady was right about the superstitious locals. 'I'm not an American tourist.'

'You'll be a dead one if you don't listen to what I'm telling you,' said Jenkins, double-checking the bolts. 'If we stay in here, it will ultimately give up and return to the wood till next May.' He muttered and picked up the discarded bat to use as a walking stick. 'I'm getting too old for phantoms and fools.'

'I can't stay in here,' said Cameron. 'My kit's outside, plus my wallet and phone. We should ring the bell in the tower—'

Jenkins shook his head. 'My grandfather took the clapper out of the only bell; he said the sound brought other things, dead things. Would you want to summon people while that thing is prowling around?'

Cameron considered the irresponsibility of his idea.

'Besides,' said Jenkins, 'except for your landlady, they all know to stay inside, no matter what is happening up here.'

Cameron watched him rub at his chest as he hobbled over to sit down next to the font. The old man continued to murmur something about 'sins of the father' and the injustice of his predicament.

'I just need to get my breath back,' he said. 'We'll be fine once the mist lifts on Ducking Day; don't worry, lad. After a few hours, it'll sleep for another year.'

'What's Ducking Day?' asked Cameron.

'The day they used to duck women in the pool for witch-craft, or rather, the last time they tried to drown the wretched souls before they found one. After that, they never risked doing so again.'

Jenkins took off his brogue shoes and rubbed at his sore ankle. After a brief time, he pointed to a recess behind an adjacent pillar.

'You'll find an inscription about the whole sorry affair over on that wall.'

The cool white-washed interior was still sweet from the spent Sunday candles, and thin sunlight shone through the dusty and cobwebbed leaded windows. They were at a high level, out of reach of feather dusters or the opportunity to peer out into the long grass and gravestones. Cameron followed the length of the short nave to the pillar displaying the sign 'Psalm 32'. He pored over the various wall plaques and antiquities, many with periods of profound local significance. The plague had hit hard at regular intervals, and civil war had decimated the village. There were memorials to those who had perished in a manor house fire and those who had died from nineteenth-century famine. The village seemed an unlucky place to live. Many of the memorials showed deaths occurring on the same date, years apart.

Today's date: Ducking Day.

He squeezed past the vacant pews with their cushioned crochet kneelers to explore the recessed area where a circular piece of dressed stone was set into the white plastered wall. Encircling the top of an epitaph, a line of webbed and dusty chain ran through four large rings. The two loose ends hung disconnected as though something was missing to complete the underside of the circle.

In memory of the innocent women of this parish cruelly taken and the hope of their ultimate salvation by the grace of God, 1644.

Below the inscription, a worn and disembodied hand plucked at a chain, worn but visible. A typed and faded slip of paper stuck to the pillar nearby showed the significance:

'THE HAND OF GOD PLUCKING THE LINK OF A CHAIN: GOD BRINGING A SOUL TO HIMSELF.'

Cameron examined the pitted length of chain that hung around the panel, threaded through the four flattened metal rings fixed to the wall. He twisted one ring to discover a woman's name engraved upon the opposite side. It reminded him of the iron object he had found near to the stone, and was of the same workmanship and age, though his find was more pitted and thinned from its time beneath the earth.

There was a clamour from the path beyond, and the sound of grave chippings being trodden by something four-legged and substantial. Cameron looked over at Jenkins, who was concerned with his injury. 'The bugger is pissing up the stones of the souls it's taken in the past,' said Jenkins, stretching off one sock. 'He does it every year to wind me up.'

'How's your ankle?' said Cameron, returning to the font.

'Twisted,' replied Jenkins, 'but that bitch's pet won't get me.'

Cameron ignored the bizarre notion. The thing outside was doubtless something rabid or manged from a distant wildlife park. At least that was what he needed to believe.

The old fellow placed a small tablet beneath his tongue and returned the pill case to his shirt pocket.

'Angina?' he asked, and Jenkins nodded, tugging on his sock and tying his shoe.

'Tell me about the women in the plaque,' said Cameron, eager to kick-start the conversation, and discover what was going on. He had made his mind up to leave the village as soon as he got back to his accommodation.

'Yes, the start of the whole miserable business,' said Jenkins. 'All of them drowned as witches down yonder.' He picked up the bat and pointed in the village's direction. Cameron had discovered the pool as he made his first sweeps earlier in the day. The open water had an unwholesome look, and the sluggish, sulphurous odour reminded him of the creature lurking in the churchyard.

He encouraged the discussion. 'Do they have something to do with the thing that chased me?'

Jenkins glanced round as if wakened from sleep. 'Yes, poor

souls, accused and drowned by the master of the hall, a long time ago now.' He held up his hand and hid his thumb, leaving four digits aloft. 'Those four links represent the poor women he hounded and murdered for his superstition. Like as not, they just resisted his advances and were condemned for it.' Jenkins looked into Cameron's face and softened his voice. 'When he went looking for his fifth, he found one.'

'What do you mean, found one?' replied Cameron.

'A bona fide, home-grown witch,' said Jenkins. 'He set her in the ducking stool, three hundred and seventy-six years to this very day. They ducked women just for minor offences like gossip or scolding, but the master used the stool as capital punishment. Tradition says she laughed at him all the way through the last rites, even as she went under the water. She was ducked twice more, and she came up both times like she was delighting in the entire business. The third time, she didn't come up at all, not from the stool at any rate.' Jenkins paused and stared at his feet, deep in thought.

'Somehow she got out of the chains that shackled her to the chair,' he said, 'but the villagers who had turned up to watch described something else. A few moments after they ducked her for the third time, there was a boiling and a steaming of the pool over the ducking stool. She streaked under the water like a torpedo and made her way to the other end of the pool. The locals were all shouting and pointing, as the witch came shrieking out of the water's edge, incensed. She turned round to the master, him being on the other side now, and curses him; "*Childless and bound will you be*," she said, or something along those lines.'

'Don't tell me he didn't have children? Not everybody wants or can have kids, even back in those times,' said Cameron.

'I know that, and stop interrupting,' said Jenkins. 'He had plenty of children, but only one legitimate, and she was up at the house, safe, or so he thought. Anyhow, the witch takes off for the avenue and runs between them old elm trees over yonder.' Jenkins raised his bat again, in the avenue's direction.

'So she slipped away?' he asked.

'Well, maybe and maybe not,' the old man continued. 'Horsemen were down by the pool, and they gave chase, but she flung herself into the long grass to hide. They followed with three hounds to the spot, and a large fox-like creature broke cover and scampered away up the ride.'

'You aren't saying she turned into a beast, and that you think she's running around outside?' said Cameron. He felt his courage returning, and he decided to take another look through the keyhole. What he thought he had seen was just his imagination from the exertion of the chase, and the mist had conjured the illusion that a larger beast had pursued him. It was likely just an escaped farm dog, big and vicious, but ultimately something that would withdraw from a determined assault. He seized the bat and Jenkins grabbed his arm. 'I'm not saying anything of the sort; she's been dead for centuries, even a witch has to die, eventually. No, it was her familiar that created the diversion. The dogs and men followed in pursuit, and the creature led them all away. They never found any one of them, but the witch came back for the master and the rest of his illegitimate offspring.'

Jenkins pulled him back into the pew. 'It's already slain many of his descendants, lying out there in the churchyard through no fault of their own. Hear me out before you do anything stupid.'

Cameron slumped onto the wooden seat, still holding the bat. 'So, this familiar devil thing, it's after illegitimate children of the old squire, every 15th of May?' he said. 'And you told me when we got that door shut it was after you?'

Jenkins nodded. 'Between this ankle and my heart,' he said. 'An eleventh-generation bastard, that's what I am, and the last. I'd have liked to sort it out, once and for all. I'm not a married man, and God knows I've been a virtuous man all my life.' He looked up at the ceiling. 'You'd think he'd just throw me a bone after all these years.'

Whatever Jenkins' curious notions about the creature outside, Cameron could sense he needed a friendly ear at this moment, even from a total stranger.

'Go on, then,' he said. 'Tell me what happened after the familiar led them away.'

'That's the darkest part of the tale. The creature runs away heading towards that dead elm at the end of the ride, though it would have been a mighty living tree then. Unbeknown to anyone present, there was a poacher in the wood close by, and he caught sight of the fox-like thing flying out of the spinney but not the horsemen. He knew about the master's scorn for such vermin, so he plots to slay the beast and take its tail to get a nice silver shilling in reward.'

'Did he shoot it then?' asked Cameron.

'Well, he shot at it and wounded it in the hind leg, but the creature limped on, as it does to this very day. He reloaded and fired again, missing the damn thing but hitting something else behind: the master's young daughter playing on the avenue and the one you saw not an hour back.'

'He killed the master's child?'

'Yes, an unfortunate accident. He didn't have time to see her on the grass, playing with a kite, so they say. He'd been so caught up with the thought of the shilling he hadn't looked where he was shooting. The master had told the housekeeper to keep the child safe in the garden when the trial began and away when the ducking began. She had slipped away and run straight out onto the avenue, just at the wrong time to get herself killed.'

'And the poacher, what did he do?'

'Poacher? He rushes over to the child, all covered in blood

down her smock, and he just stood there seized by the horror of what he had done. He sees the master coming with the remaining villagers, and he kneels, crying out he hadn't meant to do it. The master gets down off his horse and sees the man, rifle and child and puts two and two together. He takes out his pistol and blows the man's brains out.' The old man was silent for a moment.

'What, no trial or anything?' asked Cameron, shifting on the wooden pew.

'Of course not, those were different times. He killed the man, calm as could be. Poaching was a capital offence, and with the master being judge and all, it was swift justice as he saw it.'

'So the witch's curse came true, then?' said Cameron. 'About him being childless, I mean?'

Jenkins put his face in his hands. 'Yes, and no. The illegitimate children grew up and have been picked off over the years if they went anywhere near the ride. All except two.' He turned to look up at Cameron. 'My grandfather, nine times removed, and me.'

'So it's after you, then, to make good on the witch's promise?'

'Yes,' replied Jenkins. 'All the men of my line have holed up here every Ducking Day, ever vigilant, always hiding till it returns to the wood for another year and we are safe again.' Jenkins sat back and glanced up at the ceiling once more. 'I'm the last, but I'd rather go quietly if you please, Lord.'

'There must be a way to kill it, if there were enough people, I mean?' said Cameron.

'My great-grandfather tried that with soldiers returned from the Boer campaign,' he said. 'Their rifles didn't even slow it down, and the men wouldn't come back to try again once they saw it. I don't blame them.'

'You truly believe that the creature outside is a witch's

familiar, and can't be killed even by men with rifles?' said Cameron.

'We've tried gas, poison, shotguns and a bear trap. The cursed thing isn't hurt by mortal means, not anymore. This baseball bat didn't disturb it in the slightest and I hit it plenty enough times.'

'What happened to the master?' asked Cameron.

'He goes on living in the old manor house, but only for a short while before he got what was coming to him. The day after the tragedy, all the able-bodied men but the master rode out with a full pack of hounds to track down the witch and the familiar. The poacher had injured the creature, and they came upon that first, licking its hind leg. It slinked into the wood over yonder.'

Jenkins nodded towards a line of trees.

'The thing is,' whispered the old man, 'the hounds go in, nigh on thirty of them, but they don't come out. Moments later, a terrible whining and savagery echoes through the wood. The riders sound their horns thinking they've got the evil thing, but it becomes plain it's the hounds that are coming off worst in there. Not one comes back out, but something else does.'

'Our limping friend out there?'

'Yes, all bloodied and mauled but still living. It snarls at the riders and lopes off, wounded, into the dense trees on the other side where they cannot follow. They get back on their horses and go looking for their hounds, but not a sound comes out of that wood. Not far in, they find utter carnage. Dogs with throats ripped out, legs ripped off, and eyes gouged out. They even found one flung halfway up a tree.'

Cameron whistled in amazement. 'If I hadn't seen it myself, I'd have said you were pulling my leg.'

'I wish to God I was,' continued Jenkins. 'They were the

best hounds in the south of England, not easily bested or replaced.'

There was a disturbance on the tiles of the lychgate, and Cameron shot up and back to the door. He squinted through the keyhole to see the creature crouched upon the little roof, indistinct unless it shuffled in its sitting.

'It's over there on the edge of the churchyard,' he said, pulling on his coat and returning to the pew. 'So there's no way to kill it or remove it from the world while you still live?'

'I hope you're not suggesting I go out there so you can have an afternoon pint at the Horse and Hounds?'

'I don't drink,' said Cameron. 'I was thinking of a coffee instead.'

The old man broke into a grin and continued. 'No way to kill it. There was only one hound that might have stood a chance.'

Jenkins shuffled to twist sideways, ready to impart the climax of the tale. 'The fox didn't get all the dogs. There was one brute by the name of Reveral. It was as big as a pit pony, dangerous, fast and vicious. The master would feed it live fox cubs and poke at it, driving it senseless while doing so. I'm surprised it never went for him, to be honest, and why the beast put up with it when he was loose... It was only the girl he was gentle around; no one could approach but her. I guess he didn't see her as a threat. The master had an iron collar made with three valuable coins set into it for anyone brave enough to remove them from the hound's neck. Many a fool lost a full hand trying to claim them, which was likely what he intended.'

'Why was the hound spared?' asked Cameron.

'They had him locked in the kennels from the previous day, after biting his hind leg all raw and red. The master of the hounds left him behind on that fateful day, or he might have ended up the same as the rest, though perhaps not.

After the child's funeral a few days later, the master ties the hound to the old gallows post with a long chain, one hundred feet long, long enough to cover the width of the ride. Tradition says part of it hangs on the wall over there.'

'The stone socket I saw today near the top of the avenue?' said Cameron. 'It was the site of a gallows?'

'Yes,' said Jenkins, 'the post rotted away before I was born; only the stone base is left now.'

'So why was Reveral put up there?'

'To keep an eye out for the witch or the familiar, I guess,' said Jenkins, 'but we'll never know for sure. Whether the hound finally gave in and turned traitor, or someone let him go, I can't tell you, but it turns up at the house, chain and collar missing. The master goes out into the dark, brandishing a stick and shouting for peace from the noisy beast. He gets so far and sees them all there lined up, carrying the chain between them.'

'Sees who? The villagers?' asked Cameron.

'Well, what used to be villagers for sure; it was the women he had ducked, drowned or hung previous – all four of them plus the witch. The maid saw them out of the upstairs window or saw what was left of them; the incessant barking had woken her too. She only took one look and bolted her door. She said he went peaceful with them and resigned himself to fate. They wrapped the long chain around him and led him away into the night. She'd caught sight of someone else too: the ghost of the master's child up on the ride, calling for the dog.'

'Don't tell me, they found the master hanging from the gallows the next morning?' said Cameron.

'No,' said the old man. 'They didn't find him till the afternoon, a full seven hours after the maid dared to come down and tell the parson what she had seen. Wet, bloated and lifeless he was. No one had taken notice till then, but the blacksmith saw that the ducking stool was tilted forwards into the pool; it was a place folk wanted to avoid for obvious reasons that past two weeks. The villagers pushed down on it hard, and after several attempts, they got it lifted to the surface and spun round to the bank just as it snapped in two from the weight. Tied to the broken portion of the stool was the master, the massive length of his heavy iron chain wrapped around him like a spider's webbing covering all but his wide-open mouth. Something had shattered his jaw, and his mouth was stuffed with four links, each inscribed with a woman's name.' Jenkins pointed towards the memorial. 'Around his pale neck was the hound's collar, locked shut, and two of the precious coins were driven into his empty eye sockets, and could not be removed.

'No one used the stool again or got ducked, that much is true.' The old man pointed to Cameron's feet. 'They laid him out right there, and it's rare anyone sits on that spot that belongs to the village.'

Cameron shot up, looking down as if something had stung him. 'Shouldn't it have been five links they found, though, for the women he drowned?'

'No, lad. Only four are dead and gone. No one knew what happened to the fifth, but it's still linked to the village and the area somehow. The cause of all the rotten luck since, I dare say.'

Cameron thought of the link he had found, and that now lay out of reach, beyond the monster at the gate.

'The name of the witch, it wouldn't be Rose, would it?' he said.

Jenkins spun in astonishment. 'How the devil would you know that?'

'Because it's engraved on an iron ring with a split down one side that I dug up next to the gallows this morning; I took it for an agricultural bit of chain till I turned it over and saw the name.'

Jenkins stood up, wincing with the weight on his injured ankle. 'Where is it?' he asked. 'Show it to me.'

'I can't,' said Cameron, pulling out his pockets as though in proof. 'It's in my pack along with my other things, way over there on the ride. It was on the spot where the child was pointing, not long before that creature appeared.'

'You saw the master's daughter up close?' asked Jenkins, wide-eyed.

'Saw and heard her,' said Cameron. '"*Link them together,*" she said. What does that mean? Link the chain on the wall together?'

Jenkins shrugged. 'I don't know. She has never spoken to me. What do you suppose would happen if we did?'

'I don't know,' said Cameron, 'but she warned me to run when the familiar appeared, soon after I picked up the link, so I presume she's here to help. Was it trying to stop me getting to the church? You said it doesn't normally come this close.'

Jenkins hobbled to the memorial and pulled the free ends of the chain together. 'How far away is your pack?' he said, turning to Cameron.

Cameron understood the direction the conversation was about to take, though he wasn't sure who would do the running, or take the risk. 'About two hundred yards, there and back.'

'You need to create a diversion to give me a fighting chance of retrieving it,' said Jenkins. 'I'll need a few minutes, with this damn ankle.'

Cameron thought the old man was teasing him until he saw the sincere look on his face.

'You won't make it,' said Cameron, 'not in your state. I

could do it in half the time, and I know what I'm looking for. You'll need this, in case I don't make it.'

Jenkins looked at his ankle and accepted the bat from Cameron's outstretched hand.

'We need a lengthy diversion,' Cameron continued. 'As far away from the entrance as possible. You must bait it and keep it occupied from one of these windows while I slip out.'

Jenkins nodded. 'First, we need to tire it out to give you a fighting chance; let's send it round and round the church from opposite windows until it's knackered.'

The men set about stacking pews against the windows on either side. It was slow going because of Jenkins' age and his predicament. They punched holes in the leaded glass on either side, and Cameron raced up the tower and onto the roof.

The mist still clung to the ground, but he could make out the edge of the churchyard, and the rise where his pack lay, or so he hoped.

Cameron returned to see Jenkins hollering and hooting to attract the creature's attention. There was a sudden pungent stench of stagnant water, and they knew the beast was on its way. After grabbing a ceremonial staff from the altar, Cameron climbed the stack of wooden seats and smashed through several leaded diamonds in the opposite window.

'Your turn!' cried Jenkins, jabbing the makeshift weapon downwards from his safe vantage point. 'Watch it doesn't grab that staff – it will rip your arm clean from its socket.' He withdrew the bat and gave the thumbs up to Cameron, who began shouting and rattling the stone mullion of the window to attract the familiar's attention.

'It's on its way,' shouted Jenkins. 'It's working!'

Cameron heard the loose gravel outside flying from something akin to a scrambling motorcycle. The odour of the stagnant pool grew, and he braced for a sight of the beast. The thing appeared in full flight from around the western end of the tower. He could barely make it out, but it lunged at the staff protruding from the window, and Cameron kept a steady eye on the end of the staff.

'Mother of God!' he cried. 'Are you sure you don't want to get the pack after all?'

'Stop yelling and poking it,' shouted Jenkins. 'Send it back round and start counting.'

'What for?' said Cameron, pulling in the long pole. It returned splintered and considerably shorter than it had once been.

Jenkins banged the bat against his window, and the creature made off, longways around the church.

'So we can tell when it's tiring,' said Jenkins, seeking for the beast's return.

Cameron lost count of the number of times they had repeated the exploit, but one thing was clear, the time it was taking the familiar to reach him from the opposite side was growing. A dozen more times and the creature had almost doubled the journey time between the two men. He threw out the remains of the short pole and got down to the floor.

'It's time,' he said. 'If I do this, it has to be now.'

Jenkins nodded, yelling for the creature. 'I'll keep it busy as long as possible; then I'll get to the door.' The old man seemed on the verge of tears, but there was no fear in his face.

Cameron nodded in silent understanding. Here was a stranger prepared to do the extraordinary, to stop an unthinkable menace. No one was more surprised than Cameron himself as he quietly withdrew the door bolts and slipped out into the mist. He sneaked to the end of the porch and got his bearings, then took a deep breath and sprinted over the wet grass, keeping the church between himself and the window where Jenkins was baiting the familiar. He heard the man's yelling and shouting recede as he jumped the low wall, careful not to dislodge the coping stones and alert the creature. The air was unclean, and it burned in his throat as he raced towards the rise. Cameron scanned the ground in front of him, adrenaline fuelling his darting sprints back and forth.

The neck of the detector appeared first, and then his pack. He rummaged through the pockets, casting aside his mobile phone in favour of the cold metal ring.

Jenkins screamed from the open window of the church, 'It's coming! I can't get its attention back!'

The stench of the stale water grew, and the air became heavy with dew. Cameron looked up, trying to find the creature. 'It can't see you, but it's smelling for you,' shouted Jenkins.

The route back would have to be longer and through the lychgate. Even now he could hear the thing snarling and sniffing its way through the churchyard to the wall; Cameron's advantage was gone. Cameron made off at a loping pace to his right to circle the side of the church wall. He heard the familiar mount the wall; it was now in the meadow with him.

He saw the lychgate materialise and his spirits rose. The backdrop of the church loomed behind, and Cameron could see the black portal of the open church door. The indistinct figure of Jenkins stood there, bat in hand, watching but not daring to call out. Cameron met the gate to discover it was shut, and he gently lifted the latch, which gave a loud squeak. The familiar heard the sound and gave a great howl, much closer to Cameron than he had expected. There was movement thirty yards away, and he knew it had found him. Cameron raced for the open door and was only a few strides along the path when he heard the creature clatter into the gate, which had shut itself from the taught spring. Jenkins screamed in panic as it jumped the wooden hurdle and came thundering down the path in pursuit.

'Get behind the door and get ready to close it, with or without me inside!' bellowed Cameron, in full stride. He pulled back his arm and threw the link into the church ahead of him, to gift the talisman should he not make it. He dared not look round as he cast himself into the darkness.

From behind the door, Jenkins saw Cameron throw himself inside, and he closed the heavy door as fast as he could. The creature had other ideas and barged into the planed oak, thrusting open the door and forcing Jenkins into the wall. Cameron was already scooping up the link halfway down the nave as the creature recovered its wits and launched into a final sprint, ignoring the illegitimate descendant dazed behind the door. It was fortunate they had shifted the pews because there was now a straight line to the memorial and every yard would count. The air became saturated with the foul stench of the familiar skittering on the tiles of the aisle as Cameron reached the chains. He grabbed the first and slipped on the link like a carabiner and pulled the second towards it. He fumbled with the taught and heavy chains and looked round to see the horror, now fully formed, upon him. The creature lunged, gaping maw wide-open, as he shut his eyes.

The link slipped over the remaining chain.

There was a deafening toll from a bell above, and the familiar fell to the floor, rigid, as though it had been shot in full flight. It smashed into the wall beside Cameron, who darted for the pews and the safety of height. The creature rolled and shrieked as the bell continued to peal.

The chain on the wall now formed a circle around the inscription.

Jenkins limped down the aisle, calling out, but it was what

lay behind in the open doorway that caught Cameron's attention. Four ghostly figures led by a child entered the church.

'I thought you said there wasn't a working bell in the tower,' said Cameron, pulling the old man up onto the stack of pews.

'There isn't, and who the bloody hell would be ringing it?'

Jenkins noticed the spectral forms. 'It's the four women being led by the master's child,' he said, over the sound of the bell. The familiar recovered and got to its feet. It snarled and paced back and forth, cornered by the recent arrivals. The girl held up her hand, and the bell ceased. She looked behind, and the four women parted to admit something else. The men heard the slinking of a short chain being dragged by something light on its feet. They heard the panting and eager whining of the enormous hunting hound before they caught sight of it. The magnificent dog came to stand next to the child, who lifted her arm to smooth the heckles raised on its shaggy neck.

Jenkins had not exaggerated the size of the animal in his tale, and Cameron never saw a larger hound for the rest of his life. A great iron collar, finely wrought, led a long chain that lay like a serpent throughout the length of the nave.

The familiar bayed and tensed itself for the impending battle, and the girl removed her hand from the hound's neck and stabbed a finger towards it.

The hound launched itself, meeting the familiar midway in the air. They tumbled, scattering tables and hymn books, and began snapping at each other, each trying to pin the other on its back. Great gouges of flesh and blood gushed from the hound's body, but it did not relent, always striking for the lame hind leg of its rival. The familiar was stronger and faster, but was tiring at a rapid pace; the earlier chase around the church and the meadow had weakened its reserve of stamina. It withdrew from the fight, seeking to escape to the wood. Jenkins got down to close the door ahead of it, and the familiar regained his purpose, turning itself upon the old man in fulfilment of its mistress's ancient curse. It snapped and lunged at him, even as Cameron fought to pull the old man back to safety. The creature's teeth sunk into Jenkins' retreating shoe and he cried out in pain. He fell back as the familiar released, dragged back by the hound who now clung to the hind leg of its foe. Both men shuddered at the sickening crack from the vice-like jaw of the hound crunching its way through sinew and bone. The familiar turned, too late and too large to turn far enough to maul the face of its attacker. The hound wrung the leg from the creature's hip socket and the limb twisted, forcing the familiar to the ground.

'Reveral!' cried Jenkins through his agony. 'Go, boy!'

The hound launched into the air and came down upon the familiar, jaw open, pinning its neck to the floor. Reveral made to snap shut his bite when the child held up her hand to stop the kill.

The hound relented with a whimper of resentment and retreated to the girl's side.

The familiar crawled forwards, smearing the tiles with blood and bile as the four ghostly figures removed the chain from the memorial wall and bound the weakened familiar desperately trying to escape. Subdued and coiled, it cried out in mournful acceptance of its failure to fulfil the witch's curse. The four women pulled on the remaining length of chain and dragged the creature out into the mist.

Cameron removed Jenkins' shoe to reveal a single puncture wound by one of the familiar's canine teeth.

'She wants you to follow. Leave me for now – it's not serious,' said Jenkins.

Cameron glanced up, and the child beckoned him down the central aisle. At the lychgate, Cameron could see the four women dragging the creature through the meadow, and the flattened grass trail behind was making for the pool in a straight line. The mist lifted, and he saw the child and hound at the spot of his discarded detector and pack. She removed its collar, laying it on the grass beside his things, and the hound licked at her mercilessly. The hound barked, its mission complete, and she raised her hand in farewell. He heard Jenkins hobbling along the church wall, using it to compensate for his twisted ankle and bitten foot. When Cameron glanced back, the hound and the girl were gone.

Cameron retrieved his things and put his hands around the heavy iron collar. 'RV' was inscribed upon it, and he gasped at the decoration that wound around it. Three chain-mail circles were the prominent embellishment, two of them were vacant, but one of them still held its precious cargo.

He rubbed at the flat metal disc. It was a coin, and Cameron's hand trembled with the fantastic notion of what it could be. There was a kingly figure on horseback, and the view of a town between the legs of the horse, above which was stamped 'OXO'. He knew instantly what it was and the fact that only a hundred were ever minted. He turned over the coin, and the realisation of his good fortune became clear; there was the emblem of Charles I and the date, 1644.

It was a Rawlins Oxford Crown, exceptionally rare, and worth a small fortune.

He collected his things and lumbered back to show Jenkins.

'I've only ever seen one in a museum!' said Cameron, trying to extricate the treasure from its socket.

'Looks like you got your buried treasure after all,' said Jenkins. 'It'll help to pay for the damage to the glass inside, but all the blood and gore just evaporated before my eyes; I thought I was losing consciousness.' He looked down at his blood-soaked sock.

'We need to get you to the hospital,' said Cameron, shouldering his equipment and offering the man support.

'Agreed,' said Jenkins, 'but I want to follow that trail to see where it leads. I don't like leaving loose ends.'

They shuffled their way down the ride, following the flattened grass, already springing back in the bright sunshine behind them. It ended at the pool, and small bubbles of putrid air broke from the surface near its centre.

'You think it's in there, bound or drowned?' said Cameron, assisting the old man to the ground, and dialling for an ambulance.

'Let us hope so,' he said. 'I don't think we can rely on the child or the hound again. Let's believe your coin is the start of better luck for us all.'

'God threw you a bone, or rather a link of chain, after all,' said Cameron.

'And you too, finding that old coin. I wouldn't make light of where you found it, not on the ride till we are sure next year.'

Cameron nodded and opened his hand to see the coin, and the imprint of the mounted king impressed into his palm.

THE FOLLOWING YEAR, CAMERON ROSE EARLY AND MADE his way to the church by the long route. A bright, new and expensive baseball bat poked from his pack. Jenkins was already there and shuffled to meet him, exhibiting little of the limp he had gained from the encounter with the familiar. Cameron presented him with the bat, and the old man accepted it with gratitude and much humour. Jenkins' original bat was little more than a gnawed handle, but he kept it to remind him of his obligations in defending the village and the avenue on Ducking Day.

'There's no mist,' said Cameron, offering the old man a flask of tea. 'Is that significant?'

'Yes,' said Jenkins, accepting the plastic cup, 'never been like this before, in my lifetime or anyone else's. The smell has gone too.'

'I noticed that on the way up; you are safe now.'

'I'm sure of it too, but when you have lived in fear as long as I have, it's difficult to let go.'

They sat in silence for a while, and Jenkins lifted his binoculars, a Christmas gift from Cameron, to check the margins of the trees. 'Thank you for the donation to St Thomas',' he said. 'If all goes well today I will give the bell foundry the job of replacing the clapper so the tower can ring out once more.'

'I felt it my duty,' said Cameron. 'The church saved us both, and we took plenty of liberties inside. Call it an insurance policy.'

'Against what?' said Jenkins. 'Wrath of God?'

'Against me ignoring further superstitious claptrap from certain villagers I'll be living alongside,' said Cameron. 'I've bought the B&B.'

Jenkins clapped him on the back with great delight. 'Shame about that, replacing one newcomer with another,' he said, sarcastically. 'I heard the new buyer was changing the name from "Long Ride". What have you decided on, then?'

Cameron turned and winked at the old man.

'I've settled on Familiar's End,' he said, 'and I'm getting a dog, a very large dog.'

THE BOX IN THE BELFRY

I ask you to consider a tower belonging to a church in the county of Gloucestershire.

A cramped and dusty space inhabited by a cluster of bells may spring to mind. Or an antique clock mechanism perched high in a dirty chamber. To the unadventurous, or those no longer wishing to engage in the thought experiment further, then bats may rank alongside the aforementioned musical and mechanical objects.

I have visited such a place. You must be careful of your head so as not to thump into the treble or tenor bell. The dry rotten beams of Elizabethan oak appear to daze the unwary, and a veritable maze of similar obstructions make progress troublesome. Prudence with one's feet is required, and where one plans to put them. Rotten boards, trapdoor latches, mouldy old peregrine nests and rodent droppings are amongst the many treats that reside there. To the seasoned steeple keeper inspecting the condition of bells with their oak hangings and ash stays, it is paradise.

Bats were furthest from my mind as I followed my enthusiastic colleague amongst the contorted web of wood, metal and stone. I weaved around the draughty chamber like a slow-motion burglar trying to avoid trip-wired alarms. I assisted my friend in the fitting of leather mufflers to one side of the bell clappers within their giant sleeping throats. The New Year's Eve band would ring with a muted back-stroke, creating a mournful and distant companion to the typical bright and tuneful hand-stroke.

I include a fourth and fifth item for your consideration. You will acknowledge, from the ground, that the well-ventilated bell-chamber allows the joyous peal to broadcast over a wide area. Open slit windows lure the feeble-legged vertigo sufferer to ponder the tremendous height of the vantage point. It also allows an excellent opportunity to examine the water spouts, carved into grinning and grotesque gargoyles. Also on the outside, and crowning the spire, is the weathercock.

With chilling reminders of last New Year's Eve, it is the latter that will forever headline in my considerations on belfries.

DECEMBER 1931

I had received news from my best friend, William Maxwell, that his relocation to the country had gone well and that he would be glad of my company at New Year. In no particular mood to sing 'Auld Lang Syne' alone in the city, I accepted the opportunity to spend time with my fellow alumnus of King's College. I wondered how the new medicine man of the district was settling into his latest position, and I would enquire further into his hints of a blossoming romance with the vicar's daughter. He had come into custody, via the house sale, of an old journal and was interested in my opinion on its somewhat fantastical contents.

He was thrilled to hear from me, for he feared, despite my protestations to the contrary, that his house would never be worthy of someone in my position. I had always had the greatest pleasure in Maxwell's company, refuting his concern that his simple country tastes and rural interests would bore a town mouse like myself. Following intensive matters of state recently, I had retired to my chambers, slunk into my chair, and envied the pleasant working life of a country doctor. I told him so, and he had laughed down the telephone at my naivety.

'You forget the midwifery I have to do; the nearest hospital is twenty miles away.'

The very idea of being away from Parliament for a few days delighted me. In the spirit of honesty, I admit it played a very close second to seeing my old friend in his new surroundings.

I departed Paddington in thick fog on the morning of the 30th of December. To my delight, the weather broke into hazy winter sunshine after Windsor, and the pristine frozen landscape flying past the carriage window put me in a very mindful state. Maxwell had arranged my ride from the station, courtesy of a grand and expensive Daimler with a matching chauffeur. My friend was often generous beyond his means, and I resolved to repay him without causing offence when the opportunity presented itself. On my arrival at the charming ironstone house, we embraced, and he ushered me through to his firelit study. As bachelors, we spoke of many things but rarely touched on the subject of the opposite sex, but on this occasion, it was the first topic of conversation. He had become enamoured by Miss Eleanor Middleton, and he assured me that the feeling was mutual. Over a glass of ruby port, I examined his new and excitable state brought on by the vicar's daughter. I took on the role of his doctor and offered my unprofessional medical prognosis; the only remedy for his malady being a bold course of action on his part, or hers.

'My thoughts exactly!' he said. 'I have invited her and her father for dinner tomorrow evening. I hope you don't mind?'

'It will be my pleasure,' I replied, leaning over to slap my old comrade on the shoulder. 'We'll spend the evening together. You aren't planning anything rash, though?'

'No, of course not,' he spluttered, 'but you are better at this romance lark than I am. It will be a great service to me if you make certain I don't end up making a fool of myself. I'm fine talking to anyone if it's life or death, or someplace in between, but I find this whole romantic business a bit fuzzy and unscientific.'

I laughed, looking at his imploring face.

'You can relax,' I said. 'Romance will not be your principal concern tomorrow. It is the vicar you need to impress, not her.'

Maxwell held up a finger to counter my words. 'I've taken charge of the church ringing chamber, and much for the better, as the local volunteers were desperate for a competent tutor. I am in the vicar's good books with the advances in the quality of the Sunday ringing,' he said, 'and he has invited me to take on the duties of the steeple keeper, following the death of the previous volunteer.'

Maxwell had a vivacious mind, and I recalled him taking to bell ringing with both hands while at Cambridge. He was quick to learn and was soon leading other ringers in the composition or pattern known as the method. Maxwell kept every bell in position, including his own, as they weaved in and out to strike the peal. At each ringable tower in every district, he would put in as a visiting ringer, but would soon rise, because of his skill with people and ropes, as the nominated ringing master. It took little time in turning the rustic bands of ringers into a sublime musical team. On this occasion, being not only the trusted doctor for the district, and an astute and masterful ringer of bells, he was also taking on the maintenance duties of the belfry.

'I'm amazed, William,' I declared, slumping into a comfortable armchair, 'that you have any time for your patients.'

'Plenty of time for the sick and the dying,' he said. 'Most of the call-outs suffer from an acute bout of curiosity to see the new general practitioner.'

He unlocked a bookcase on the opposite wall and retrieved a tattered card-bound folio.

'Is that the journal you mentioned? The one with a queer tale in it?' I said.

'Yes,' he replied. 'It's an entire working history of the belfry, going back a hundred years and written by scores of past keepers. It's interesting, to me at least, and I wonder whether I should continue the tradition?' He handed me several loose sheets.

'I'm dammed if I know what a steeple keeper does,' I enquired, glancing at the bold, handwritten entries. There was a date above each one, followed by the works and inspections carried out.

Sometimes, even amongst one's dearest friends, you wish you had not enquired on a subject for which you only required a brief answer. I endured a full ten-minute treatise on the necessary poking, prodding and maintenance of the belfry that kept the bells swinging and in good order. Still talking, he refilled my glass several times and dwelled on the historical lack of care in the current tower of St Luke's.

'Look at this entry from Richard Deveral, the former steeple keeper. It's incomplete, unfortunately,' he said. 'I hope you still enjoy ghost tales.'

We had both been members of the Chit-Chat Club for Old Etonians while at Cambridge. Here we had been chilled by the masterful ghost stories of the provost who had performed his pleasing terrors to us at the darkest time of the year. I looked into the fire, its light glinting on my crystal wineglass, and recalled the candlelit companionship and the supernatural tales recounted in that comfortable room long ago.

I never thought I would live through a ghost story of my own.

William refilled my glass with the full-bodied claret that he had been saving and could ill-afford. I glanced at the remaining words on the torn entry:

I dare not open it again, not even to entomb it back in its rightful place on the steeple. The blacksmith will not entertain working on it for fear of injuring the creature or himself. What have we done?

It appears benign, and the records attest that the spire has never in recorded history been struck by lightning or endured any misadventure. The simple beliefs of the area ascribe a beneficial or guardian spirit to reside even within the simplest of weathercocks, and I am of the mind that these superstitions may have some basis in truth and that the thing is a shield against tempests and storms. It has a degree of physical form and scratches most unsettlingly in the belfry above, causing disquiet and talk of vermin amongst the congregation who are blessedly ignorant of its origin or nature.

God bless the tower and all those who ring within it.

R.D.

I LAID DOWN THE TATTERED PAGE AND GLANCED UP AT Maxwell, bright-eyed and beaming.

'Quite a disquieting tale for a winter's eve,' I said, 'and the beginning is missing if there is one. Is this Richard Deveral character alive?'

'No, he died recently in this house, I understand, and left the folio as part of the contents,' he replied. 'I've been waiting for an opportunity to have a good look and see if there is anything up there, even though it's likely nonsense brought on by bells and ale; the two frequently go together.'

'I don't believe in spirits,' I said, 'and you recall I hate heights, but I will humour you for more of that claret. You're positive there is no more of the story?' I leafed through the remaining scripts.

'Nothing in the other sheets and I've been through all the trunks,' he said. 'There's nothing further to discover unless you want to enquire at the inn; he spent much time there, apparently.'

'Perhaps it's an inside joke?'

'Well, why don't you come with me to the tower tomorrow and we'll investigate,' he said. 'I need to get the treble bell ringing smoothly again before the service on New Year's Eve, and you can give me a few pointers on impressing Eleanor.'

He lifted his eyebrows and waited for my affirmation. A dusty chamber of bats and bells would be an unusual but private place to advise him on matters of the heart. I raised my glass in a toast to doctors and their curious pastimes.

'Best give me a pair of your old flannels and take some of this up there to keep us company,' I said, before draining the last of my claret and retiring to my room.

WHEN I AWOKE THE FOLLOWING MORNING, THERE WAS ringing in my ears. I fumbled with the alarm clock and lay back, listening to the tick-tock and a few sparrows welcoming the dawn beyond the light gauze curtains. Maxwell was waiting downstairs, stealing breakfast from the housekeeper as she attempted to set the table.

'I need to make a few house calls before we head to St Luke's. I wonder if you would like to see a bit of the town while I am at it,' he said, munching a mouthful of marmalade toast. 'Nothing serious, just a few characters to check on. After that, I can give you a tour of the belfry. We could lunch at the Fleece Inn if your stomach needs settling after the excitement.'

I did not acknowledge my discomfort about visiting the belfry, but nodded and accepted the itinerary. A bracing walk with the new doctor would confirm my conjecture that my envy regarding his occupation was justified. A short and reluctant poke about a dusty chamber followed by a good hearty lunch at the local inn would be a satisfactory prelude to meeting Miss Middleton and the vicar later that day.

'There are queer old things inside the Fleece too,' he declared, over biscuits and bacon. 'You can enquire about the unquiet spirit if you like.'

I'd all but forgotten the fantastical tale from the previous evening.

'You mean there's a poltergeist about the inn?' I said.

'No, I meant the tower and the entry from Deveral last night,' said Maxwell, pushing his plate away. 'I'm a staunch believer in the scientific method, and my money is on a hallucinatory state, some herbal concoction put into the man's beer, I'll warrant.'

It seemed a rational explanation as I glanced out of the window on the crisp, bright morning, though the entry mentioned a congregation of people below, unnerved by the scratching in the tower. They couldn't all be suffering from delusion.

Maxwell got up and included two sets of old clothes to his mobile Gladstone bag apothecary. He made several phone calls while I stole a swift glance at the newspapers. Ready for my excursion around the local area, we picked up a hip flask and walking stick apiece and headed out into the lane. As we walked, he outlined various architectural features of the small market town that interested me.

'Is that your blessed steeple?' I interrupted, pointing to the distant honey-coloured spire, framed between several mock Tudor houses.

'Yes, that's St Luke's. Bizarre weathercock on the top, don't you think? You can see it for miles.'

From a distance, the weathervane and its great golden serpent-like ornament stood out, marking the church and the wind direction. A well-dressed couple acknowledged us and enquired as to the doctor's health. While I pondered the irony, the vane swung to the east, and the watery sunlight glinted across its entire profile. I perceived that while I was correct in my initial conclusion that the head of the beast was beaked, the rest of the body was far more sinuous and monstrous than a serpent.

Pleasantries exchanged, we marched on to the centre of town.

'Curious creature for the top of a church,' I mentioned, pointing my stick to the steeple top. 'Some sort of serpent or basilisk?'

Maxwell halted and squinted, shielding his eyes from the low morning sun. 'Yes, I suppose you're right. Rather an odd beast to be the guardian of the tower.'

'You don't believe in that nonsense from last night?' I asked. 'Why would a church defended by God need additional protection?'

Maxwell slowed. 'There's no rationale to superstition, but I presume it's keeping the bells in order or protecting them from lightning. I appreciate you are excited about such things, but wait till you see the belfry! There are many curious carvings up there, original medieval gargoyles mostly, and you won't find those on your Neo-Gothic parliament building.'

'The vane looks newer than the church,' I said, as we turned down a narrow side street for the first of Maxwell's brief appointments.

'Yes, I noticed that,' he said. 'I asked the verger about it when I arrived. He confirmed they installed the new vane at the turn of the century; the old one was all but rust and held together by faith, allegedly.' He chuckled and wrapped the brass knocker of a polished front door.

'The tenor bell fell silent around that time; it's been out of service because of the dry rot in the frame. There's a substantial hairline crack in its lower section too. I was hoping we might launch a fund to get all six back to full muster.'

Two doors later, after several re-dressed wounds, and a bottle of gripe water for the grocer's teething toddler, we headed towards St Luke's. A handsome row of smooth snakebark cherry trees lined the approach, and beyond these Maxwell paused. He grasped the top of the iron railings and studied the modest Queen Anne period vicarage.

It was a quaint old place, with overgrown wisteria hanging from the frosted brickwork. Spent and seeding anemones littered the borders, and the spicy fragrance of winter jasmine peppered each frosty inhalation. The dark windows showed no trace of habitation, as Maxwell confirmed. He informed me that the vicar superintended several other churches of the district, and both the Middletons were out and about. He turned to accompany me along the frozen gravel path of the well-tended graveyard. When we reached the church porch, Maxwell swung open the massive iron-studded oak door. My eyes became accustomed to the low light, and he made off to the sacristy to change. I took my time wandering past the Victorian reproduction pews, bedazzled by the light streaming through the pre-Reformation painted glass and onto the polished flagstone memorials. The empty church was serene now that the Christmas festivities were over. At the altar, there was a carved wooden nativity scene illuminated by large puddles of pure white sunlight beaming in from the cobwebbed, leaded windows. Desiccated holly curled on hymn-book-laden tables, and the smell of candles and incense lingered in testimony to the services of the preceding week. My footsteps resounded as I made my way to the back of the church, wafting vast glittery swarms of dust motes behind me. At the rear, and right beneath the tower, I poked my nose through the heavy crimson curtains hiding the ground floor ringing chamber. Five bell ropes dominated the otherwise empty room. The cotton-striped 'sallies' hung from a raised central wooden disc, suspended in the centre of the ceiling, making the place look like the skeleton of a Bedouin tent.

'Plenty of time to teach you to ring,' said Maxwell.

I closed the curtains and turned to see him in his old clothes.

'You have been trying to get me into your obsession for years, William,' I replied. 'Be grateful that my trip to a cold belfry will only cost you lunch.'

I changed into an enormous pair of farm overalls and ended up having to roll the legs to avoid tripping on the narrow treads of the spiral staircase leading to the bell chamber. After an awkward and trying few minutes in confined spaces, the steps ended at the roof of the square tower. Maxwell took out a key and unlocked the small door, yanking it inward with a blast of frigid air. The breeze was much stiffer up here and bit at our faces as we traversed around two sides to reach a small portal that would lead us into the belfry. I caught brief glimpses of the bells sleeping in the gloomy chamber and peered across at the charming chimney-filled scene of the Cotswolds beyond. Maxwell was already on his hands, squirming his way through the little hatch when the sudden creak of the weathercock, thirty feet above, startled me. A wave of nauseous vertigo took hold as I peered up at the intricate burnished metal, decorated and skilfully engraved. The artisan who had crafted this showed exceptional skill in creating a remarkably detailed representation of a mythical beast. It was visible for many miles, but at a very much reduced resolution to the curious piece I was studying at close range. I stared down to see Maxwell's head as it emerged through my legs, back through the opening. He called for me to follow, and I gingerly squeezed my way through into the belfry. I stood up to head height between two interlocking beams covered with carpenters' marks and other deep and somewhat more recent scratches.

'Yes,' said Maxwell, 'weird, aren't they? I wondered about them too, but nothing in the journal mentions what they are. There are more by the window.'

I gathered my bearings quickly in the compact space. Maxwell ducked under the axle of the clock mechanism and made his way around to the largest of the bells on the dusty floor. It no longer hung amongst its ancient brethren. I mirrored his pathway and glanced down on the headstock of the great bell.

'Well, here's the tenor, and sadly not where it should be,' he said, showing the vacant space amongst the cluster of cart-wheels that held the other bells.

'I can see the crack you told me about from here,' I said, getting down on my haunches for a closer view in the dim light.

'There are grooves outside, too,' said Maxwell, pointing to

the opposite side. 'I'll get to work, and then we can have a scout around.'

I ran my hand over the grooves. They were a few inches long, running in groups of three or four parallel lines. One mark ran through the raised letter W of Whitechapel, the foundry that had given fiery birth to the enormous bell over a century ago.

'Some corrosion, perhaps?' I said as Maxwell preoccupied himself with fitting the sound-deadening mufflers for the New Year's Eve service.

He opened an oil-skinned leather bag nearby and took out five broad leather pads, each with a leather thong. He fixed each muffler to the striking side of each clapper that dangled expectantly like a blackbird chick waiting for its worm.

I passed him a grease gun and large spanner; he got to work checking all the swinging mechanisms. Outside, the thin clouds parted, and sunlight tiptoed in through the eastern window.

'If you stick your head out and peer down to the left and right,' Maxwell said, booming from the throat of the treble bell, 'you'll see those gargoyles I was telling you about.'

After bending and buckling my way to the slender and breezy slats, I put my feet within the spokes of the broken ringing wheel, lying disused on the dusty floor. I gripped the central mullion and leaned through the opening into the chill winter air. It was barely wide enough, and my ears brushed against the crumbling sandstone uprights. I was aware of how ludicrous I may have appeared from the ground to onlookers, but this feeling changed to one of apprehension when I twisted to look left.

At each of the angles near the base of the spire, there were weather-worn but discernible gargoyles. I stared at the wicked tongue lolling and salivating with the drip-drip of melting grime from the run-off from the steeple sides. A frigid blast of air woke me; I tore my gaze from the gargoyle's timeless stare, and I turned to the right to consider its south-easterly companion, replete with comical birds' nest hair. My sense of unease, being so high, was diminishing when a landing pigeon startled itself and me. I stumbled backwards, grazing my ears, and landed on my back. I narrowly missed clanging my head on a nearby bell.

'You all right?' said Maxwell, finishing his works.

I lay still and rubbed my burning ears.

That's when I saw it.

From my prostrate vantage point facing the underside of the low beam, I could see a small rectangular shape protruding from the oak that enveloped it. Maxwell came round to check I hadn't banged myself senseless during my hasty withdrawal from the window. He followed my pointed finger and bent beneath the beam, running his hands over the letterbox-shaped object.

'What the devil is it?' he asked, seeking the edges to pull the object from its mooring.

I drew out my silver flask, and he returned a look of surprise when I neglected to drink from it. I intercepted a thin ray of sunshine from the east window and redirected it to where Maxwell was having some success dislodging what turned out to be a narrow box. He grinned at my schoolboy trick, and it wasn't long before he had the rectangular object in the palm of his hand. He polished the visible face of the object on his trousers, like a village cricket captain shining a cherry red cricket ball. The exquisitely made box was intricate with scarce enough room to store a fountain pen. It had tiny marquetry pieces, and we scrutinised it by the light of the window louvres, concluding it was fabricated from contrasting and expensive African hardwoods. No lid or opening mechanism could we identify, and several attempts to open it were unsuccessful. Maxwell shook the box, and it rattled as though containing small dice and sand.

'The guardian of the tower is smiling on us,' I said, 'but what's in it?'

'Jewels and pearls, by the sound of it,' joked Maxwell. 'Let's get cleaned up and head over to the inn; we can examine it at our leisure.'

To this, I agreed. In the mirrored light of the flask, I double-checked the hole, feeling inside with my fingers. It was smooth but still held the tacky resinous substance that once secured the box in the belfry. What I noticed, however, were parallel scratch marks, like those on the tenor bell. They circled the opening, and if I had seen these first, I doubt I would have inserted my hand where the sunlight could never reach.

WE RETRACED OUR STEPS BACK TO THE SACRISTY AND washed our grubby hands in the cracked butler's sink. We changed clothes, and Maxwell rubbed some stinging witch-hazel ointment into my ears to lessen the bruising, leaving a warm red glow about the lobes. Gladstone bag and sticks in hand, we left the church behind with the box snug against the flask in my friend's breast pocket.

We strolled back through the outskirts, one of us at least content to be outside.

It was midday, and the Fleece Inn was all but deserted on account of it being market day in the neighbouring town. A moss-pimpled thatched roof covered the small leaded windows like wizened eyebrows, and masses of rose hips and old man's beard sprawled in front of the white-washed daub. I sampled the local ale and the hock of ham that Maxwell had prescribed, then relaxed back into my chair while he took out the wooden box.

I lit a cigarette with a long taper from the smoky fire. Three worn white rings, a foot in width, had been painted on the hearthstones.

'I haven't seen these before,' I said. 'In London or anywhere else, before you mention it.'

Maxwell glanced over at the circles. 'Yes, some curious things here.'

He was about to explain when the landlord appeared and cleared away the table. Maxwell urged the man to recount the tale that he had heard several months prior, on his first visit to the establishment. The landlord began but looked a little embarrassed to be telling what he considered a local superstition to a stranger. Maxwell encouraged him to continue despite his hesitation about discussing the matter with such a learned gentleman.

'Those are witches' circles, sir,' he said. 'In olden days they warded off curses and spirits, they say. Nothing bad gets into the inn through the open chimney, and we let nothing unnatural in through the door.'

'There are a few witches' marks on the beams as well, aren't there?' added Maxwell, now testing what he believed to be the lid of the box with the blunt end of a butter knife.

'Yes, sir. If you have the time, I'll show them to you. They are in the lintels to keep anything that got in from moving about,' said the landlord. 'I'm a modern thinking man, and I don't hold with the simple tales of the past, but it puts me in mind of the queer happenings with Mr Deveral during my grandfather's time, after which he had me paint them circles afresh when I was just a lad.'

I urged him to continue, hoping he would shed more light on the mysterious goings-on written in the journal, without me enquiring about them. I saw Maxwell wink, and he put on a wry smile as he sought to open the box.

The story was brief but described curious knockings and banging within this very room when the present landlord was but a child. As a boy, he had been tending the fire when the steeple keeper had entered the taproom bearing the old weathervane from the church tower. The steeplejack had removed it that morning, and it needed considerable attention from the blacksmith who patronised the place when not at his forge. Still sober, and being of sudden mind, he took to drawing and poring over the works needed, putting together a rough idea of cost and time involved to fabricate a close replica. He was an able man but would have difficulty repairing the small and hollow globe onto which the strange weathervane creature turned. The thin brass sphere was much corroded and cracked open during the examination, spilling its '*bits of bones*'.

Maxwell looked up. 'Bits of bones?'

'Well, yes, sir. I recall because I had a darn good hiding from my old man for what followed, and I swear on my barrels I had nothing to do with it.'

I encouraged him to continue. 'What was in the sphere?'

'Bones and dust, sir,' the landlord replied. 'I know because my father had a magnifying glass for reading precious metal marks, him being interested in old watches.'

'It was a reliquary?' I asked.

The landlord scratched his head. 'I don't know about that, sir, but I was standing right here, and the chimney blew one hell of a smoke and soot back into the room. My eyes stung, and the thing from the sphere whistled back down and put the fire out.'

There was a pause. Maxwell and I waited for some conclusion or explanation. He saw our expectant and honest enthusiasm and continued.

'It wasn't something coming into the inn from the chimney,' he said. 'It was something trying to get back out, if you take my word, and having right trouble doing so on account of the circles...'

'Something?' we both said in unison.

The landlord moved over to the crooked diamond-leaded window on the opposite side of the room and wrung his hands. 'The thing, whatever it was, took off into the taproom and banged around under those marks till it whirled back like a tempest, followed by Mr Deveral and my father wielding a truncheon.'

He pointed to a small and replaced section of glass. Not recent, but of this century.

'It came flying back in here, bouncing off the pewter plates before bursting through this here pane.'

Maxwell stared at me, and I was sceptical whether he sought to goad me into laughter. The landlord, however, appeared to my astute eye to be telling the truth, albeit one that had embellished itself in the recounting over the years.

'What do you put this manifestation down to?' I asked.

'Well, it's plain enough that whatever was in that sphere got free somehow, and Mr Deveral knew it. He swept up the bits and took them away with him in a wrapped cloth. Call it what you will, but I had a striking in front of both of them for breaking that glass. My father had a cruel temper, and he was in no mood for nonsense. He accused me of playing ball or some such game and made me clear up all the mess; I only found a few pieces on the floor, snivelling as I was.'

'There were more fragments on the outside?' I added.

The landlord raised his eyebrows. 'Yes, sir. Whatever it was came bursting out from the inside, but not from me. A few days later, Mr Deveral returned, and there was quiet talk with my grandfather. Soon after, he had me painting these witch circles afresh with white lime. My father had a rare moment of softness and felt somewhat guilty of his rough treatment to me, and I got myself a brand-new cricket bat out of it. It hangs above the bar area for all to see; I scored a few runs for the town with that.'

'Did they find out what it was or catch it?' asked Maxwell.

'I believe so. My father tells me they lured it into the church tower and the bells of St Luke's sent the thing to sleep. With the aid of the vicar and the blacksmith, he trapped it under the tenor bell, recently off its wheel. I eavesdropped the night they came back, shaking and drinking strong whisky on account of the adventure.'

I felt uneasy knowing I had been alongside the metal prison of the bell, even in a yarn as spun out as this one. 'Are you suggesting it's still under there?' I said.

'No, but where it went to, or what they did with it, they wouldn't say.'

I agreed it was a remarkable tale, and he collected our plates and disappeared into the other room. I studied Maxwell, who had given up with the box and was peering down at the faded circles.

'Thank you for putting him up to it, William,' I said. 'I half believed him for a moment.'

Maxwell looked up and drained his glass. 'I didn't put him up to anything, and it's the first I've heard of the entire business. He only told me there was a ghost that broke windows, but I can see the yarn improves in the retelling.'

I left with my thanks for the food and the curious tale, and I noticed the well-used willow bat above the bar.

There was some greater mystery, and I reflected upon it as I blew on my hands with my hot breath. Maxwell was inside settling the bill. I navigated through an overgrown flower border to examine the replaced piece of glass, half expecting to see them both inside, rolling with laughter at my expense. The room was unoccupied, but the windowsill had deeply incised sets of parallel grooves, like those in the tower.

WE MADE OUR WAY BACK INTO TOWN, STOPPING TO purchase a bottle of port for after dinner. At the butcher's, we collided with the housekeeper, out provisioning for the meal. As an apology, we became porters for the bags and boxes, which the poor woman would have had to revisit later.

She marched ahead to collect even more, but these were smaller items. It gave Maxwell time to think on the evening, and he mentioned how much he was looking forward to entertaining his first dinner guests. He had spent an age deciding on a highly decorated hatpin he had bought for Miss Middleton as a token of his affection. On our return, the housekeeper (now cook) bustled her way around the humble kitchen and dining room. She urged us both out of the kitchen, and we decamped to the snug. After a rapid game of patience, I withdrew to my room to renew my examination of the newspaper and its cryptic crossword. Maxwell was cleaning off the box, hoping to make some discovery to aid in its opening.

It was not so very long when, through a mild doze, I woke sharply to the echo of Maxwell calling out, accompanied by several thumps beneath the floorboards. I rushed downstairs to the shriek of the panicked housekeeper and saw Maxwell opening one of the sash windows. He shouted for her to get out; she did not need telling twice. I edged in, missing the woman as she hurried back into the kitchen, locking the door behind her for good measure.

'What the hell is going on, William?' I said, out of breath. 'Are you all right?'

Something brushed past my tender ear and rushed out of

the window, dragging the light curtains with it. Maxwell pulled them back through and slammed the sash down with such force I thought the glass would break. He drew the curtains leaving a slit which he peeped out of, panting heavily. I was about to ask again when I noticed the small box and its spilt contents; the lid lay on the floor, ten feet away. I turned on the light, listening to my friend muttering to himself, and examined the box and the detritus spewed across the polished mahogany desk. There was dust, lots of it, plus dark, gritty pieces of what looked like volcanic glass or sand. There were also, without doubt, minor pieces of yellowed teeth or bone. The dust lay like some ejecta from an impact crater. This, however, was no impact, and Maxwell scouted through the slit, then turned back to answer me.

'You won't believe this,' he said. 'The creature that broke the glass at the inn...'

'It was in the box?' I said, picking up the parts and setting them back on the table.

'Yes, I'd just managed to prise the lid off, and the thing just erupted, scattering the contents all over the place. I can't believe it.' He ran over and gripped me by the arm for comfort. 'What the hell have I done?'

Here we were, repeating history, and the opening line of the journal entry struck me:

I dare not open it again, not even to entomb it back in its rightful place on the steeple ... What have we done?

'It seems to have gone, whatever it was, for now. I'll get you something for the shock and check on the housekeeper.'

He nodded and slumped into an armchair; it was then I noted a slight cut on his cheek. 'I'll fetch your bag; you need to clean that up,' I said, pointing to the weeping scratch.

I NEGOTIATED WITH THE FRIGHTENED WOMAN TO UNLOCK the door to the kitchen. She had barricaded herself in and took to the brandy bottle for her nerves. She believed that a small bat had got into the room, making a frightful din as it banged and crashed its way into the picture rail and mirror. The doctor had opened the window as she fled. I did not chastise the poor woman for her fear of bats when my apprehension was rising. I assured her it was now out of the house and returned to Maxwell, seated and shaking, with a glass of brandy of his own.

'Are you all right?' I said, closing the door behind me and opening his medical bag.

'Yes, just a little shaken. Is she...?'

'She thinks it's a bat and I've reinforced the assumption. The question is, what do you think it was?'

'I don't believe in coincidences, and I am a scientifically minded man, not prone to fantasies. I don't know what to think at the moment, only that it would have been best, in hindsight, to leave things be considering Deveral's entry and the tale from the landlord.' He looked over at the pieces of the box. 'Why did I have to open the damn thing?'

'Did you get a look at it?' I asked.

'Yes, and no. When I prized the lid off, the thing burst free, scratching me on the face. The dust had given it form, and I saw enough to determine that it's a smaller version of that creature on top of the spire. That's when I cried out. By the time the housekeeper came in, it was clear of its covering and became difficult to follow, but not entirely. It's quick, like a weasel that can fly; I've encountered nothing like it.'

Maxwell got up and put down his glass, pointing to a few smudge marks on the ceiling.

'That's where it bashed itself about; I thought it would knock itself senseless trying to escape.'

I pressed him on the shoulder and reminded him of his

good sense to have opened the window, with little time to consider. I cleaned the cut, and Maxwell applied a stinging antiseptic.

It was then we heard the most horrifying scratching noise on the roof tiles. Maxwell had recovered his wits and ran to the fireplace, snapping shut the chimney draught.

'Whatever it is,' I said, 'we need to get it back in its box and return it to the belfry.'

Maxwell gave me a look of horror.

'I destroyed the box getting it open, and it's made of some holy wood or other to keep it in.' He pointed to the myriad of tiny wooden pieces on the floor that I had missed. The thing on the roof slithered through the chimney pot and scraped its way down the chimney.

'It's trying to get back in! We don't have any of those witch marks like the inn,' he said glancing over at the ashen fragments on the table. 'It's coming back for those bits of bone.'

The creature was dislodging pieces of loose fire cement on its travels. I grabbed the nearby poker. It tapped and scraped its way around the opposite side of the metal shutter. The distant clock tower struck four times, and the bells subdued the creature. I banged on the underside sheet metal with the iron rod, which resonated throughout the room; the thing beyond became passive. A last echo of the bells receded, and the thing stirred once more.

It climbed back up the narrow flue, scraping the brick-work and showering the metal shutter with grit and soot.

We needed a plan, and I glanced through the slit in the curtains at the distant outhouse. There was a brief window of opportunity. If I could get to the outhouse with what remained of the box and its contents, the creature would follow. For the time being, it would ease the worry; we would have the thing elsewhere until we came up with a better long-term solution or sought aid. Maxwell considered the evening plans and agreed. To his credit, he drew back the curtains and opened the window, before preparing to step into the garden before I called him back.

'I'm the quicker runner, and if anything happens to me, at least there is a doctor in the house,' I said. I drained the rest of his brandy for luck and courage.

Maxwell stared at me, relieved by the outcome of my common sense, and swept up the pieces and dust into his handkerchief. I moved closer to the chimney to test my theory and held the bundle at arm's length within the fireplace.

The creature turned and headed back down to the shutter.

'I must be quick,' I said, 'but not so quick that you can't get a good look at it. At the worst, I'll just throw it in the bushes. You need to stay here and let me know how close it gets. Make sure you close the window if I don't get back for any reason.'

Maxwell grasped my arm, unable to express verbally the concern for what I was about to undertake.

'Don't worry, William,' I said. 'We can't have this business clouding your first official engagement with Miss Middleton.'

He slapped me on the back as I launched out of the window and across the rime-frosted lawn. The brick and tiled outhouse was only one hundred yards away, by the boundary of the hedge.

I did not look back. I began my sprint over the frozen grass, and I was halfway to the dilapidated building when I heard Maxwell call out behind me.

'It's coming!' he cried.

I did not require any further encouragement and darted across the remaining yards to the outhouse door, praying that it was unlocked. A moment later I was there, rattling the rusted latch feverishly, trying to gain access, working to force it ajar, and cast the object of the creature's desire within.

I heard the thing claw its way out of the chimney, scratching the clay fire pots like fingernails on a blackboard.

I barged into the cluttered room, full of garden chairs, bric-a-brac and tools, and realised my plan was flawed.

Maxwell was yelling and pointing to the lawn. The creature was slithering towards the outhouse and carving the frost thirty yards away. It was upon me, but it jumped up onto the tiled roof and began skidding about, making its way down to the door. Realising with horror that I would meet it on my exit if I could not find another opening, I clambered over to the cobwebbed window, trying to force it open.

I heard Maxwell's approaching footsteps and fervent cry, 'For God's sake get out of there!'

I gave the stubborn window one final thump with the flat of my palm, and it flew open. I cast the wrapped bundle into a box of oily hessian rags and launched myself through the open frame. I narrowly missed Maxwell swinging at the creature with an iron poker in one hand, and a burning brand in the other. The thing retreated through the door and was now inside, colliding with various tins and jars, and setting the paraffin lamps swinging. I slammed the door behind it, and several of the lanterns fell onto the tinder-dry reeded floor, spilling their flammable contents. Maxwell pulled me back and threw the lit brand through the window before wedging it shut. The floor erupted into flame, and we felt the sudden blast of heat from several feet away. The crazed banging within the burning building intensified as the creature sought to escape. It thudded once upon the toughened glass, and I saw it uncloaked, wreathed in shadow and flame. It was a thing of turbulent horror.

'Look to the door!' he said. 'It can't get out this way. There's a mark on the frame – it's reclaimed from an earlier building.' He pointed to an engraved mark on the lintel, a witch's mark.

Maxwell was there first, holding back insistent and desperate thuds from within. I got the latch down and wedged his discarded iron bar through the hole of a missing padlock. We both leaned our backs against the door until the smoke and heat became too much. The banging weakened and stopped. A dreadful death cry akin to that of a tormented bird of prey coincided with the collapse of the tiled roof inwards, sending a shower of sparks into the winter sky.

The housekeeper came running out to meet us, and she was puzzled when Maxwell refused to call the fire station. The blaze was under control, and we were both happy to see the matter remain so. She had heard Maxwell shouting from within once again, and the brave woman, bolstered by the brandy, had left the house despite her fear of bats. We stood by and watched the fire from the safety of Maxwell's fishpond for a full twenty minutes until we were both satisfied that the creature was gone, interred, or dead.

WE AIRED THE HOUSE BUT LIT NO FIRE, AND THE SHUTTER remained firmly closed for many days. The housekeeper's husband arrived to manage the smouldering ruin and was unaware of any smoke or odour lingering in the snug. The retired handyman had looked after the bit of garden at the back, and it was fortunate that he had sent away the mechanical mower for service. He was able to rebuild and extend the building in the spring, but not after Maxwell had made a thorough investigation of the charred ash and remains. The handyman refitted the collapsed stone lintel containing the witch's mark, on account of its historical significance, and he promised to keep a close eye on the improved security door with its double padlock. We both knew that the thing was no more, but a secure building protects against many things and provides restful sleep for those with secrets.

The evening passed most pleasurably and without further incident. The Middletons arrived, and the bright and cheery conversation clouded over much of the afternoon's travails. Eleanor Middleton, whom William had underrated, exchanged many flirtatious glances with the doctor, before enquiring at some length about the deep cut upon his cheek. Rather than making a fool of himself, he performed admirably; the shock of the previous few hours had impaired his tendency to say the first thing that came to mind.

They were both saddened to learn of our earlier misadventures, and we stared at the silhouette of the handyman, back-lit by the smouldering fire. He leaned on the rake until the housekeeper collected him and left us all with best wishes for the New Year. I embellished our adventurous afternoon by recounting the monstrous bat which had made its way into the outbuilding. I had foolishly dropped my cigarette, which caused the fire, and regaled Miss Middleton, who was wide-eyed in admiration, with how Maxwell had discovered that the wooden door had clicked shut behind me. He had forced the window open and heroically dragged me into the open air, coughing and spluttering. The roof had collapsed moments later, and I owed my life to my blushing friend sitting opposite. Caught between the admiring gaze of the young lady he held in high affection and the urge to refute my white lies, he settled for a light tap against my shin beneath the table.

I saw him silently mouth the words '*I owe you.*'

We left Maxwell and Miss Middleton in the dining room, while the vicar and I continued our discussions in the snug. I peered out of the garden-facing window to see the barely discernible glow of the outhouse.

I asked him whether any old records or diaries of his forebears existed that might mention the steeple restorations around forty years prior. He promised to look into the volumes in his library, many of which were copies of earlier works. His forebear had been a prolific scribe and recorder of everyday comings and goings and he surmised that there would likely be some mention of it. He had no interest personally but would encourage Maxwell to look at his leisure.

'I would like to support a fund for the new tenor bell,' I said, as we sat down in the two comfortable armchairs, 'and provide for a lightning conductor to protect the tower.'

'My dear sir!' said the vicar, barely able to contain his excitement and joy. 'That is most wonderful news. Mr Maxwell has spoken of you as a man of generous spirit, and your position in Parliament would suggest access to wealthy benefactors.'

I held out my hand to limit the praise. 'I would ask that this remain in the strictest confidence between us, as I wish to provide for these two expenditures anonymously.' The vicar looked a little surprised at my emphasis on the last word, but relaxed into a smile. 'God sees all, my friend,' he said.

'That is just what I am hoping for,' I said, cryptically. 'I would like to repay a friendship of many years, and Maxwell's refusal to accept reimbursement for the outhouse has left me at an honourable disadvantage.'

The vicar nodded and leaned forwards to pat me on the hand. 'It would appear we have a new guardian of the tower.'

'How so?' I snapped, not realising his meaning.

'Only that we should lose the spire and our beloved bells should ever lightning strike with that monstrous vane acting as a perfect conductor.' He extended his hand, and I shook it warmly. 'I agree to your terms,' he said, 'though your friend will suspect you with no inference from me.'

An hour later, we left the house, well-wrapped for the service and the ringing in of the New Year. Maxwell and Miss Middleton walked ahead, and the vicar and I were glad to see them arm in arm. A bright new pin adorned her hat.

Despite my apprehension of entering the church again, it was a happy and jolly place, full of townsfolk and cheerful expectation. A great wave of hope and optimism that strikes people at this time of year has never now left me. Maxwell and his band of ringers rang an immaculate touch of 'Grandsire Doubles' on the remaining bells, and I sat listening to the sweet and muffled sounds from the tower. I imagined the dark and lonely belfry, missing its guardian spirit, and I resolved, for the New Year and beyond, to never visit such a place ever again.

Our curiosity had few consequences for both of us unless it was my outlook on life afterwards. Saddened by the death, albeit unintentionally, of a creature we knew nothing about, I could not shake the guilt that our ignorance had removed it from the world, and the feeling that it had a beneficial reason for existence. A line from the torn journal often came to my thoughts when I looked at some unfamiliar church from a distance:

It appears benign...

MAXWELL PROPOSED TO MISS MIDDLETON THE FOLLOWING June. I transferred the money and returned to see the new bell installed. I looked up through the ringing chamber hatch to see that the underside of the old bell being lowered was far more damaged than it had suggested sitting in the belfry. Maxwell and I both noted the parallel grooves and scratches covering the insides. Maxwell held up his hand to halt the ropes at head height, and he examined the marks. To my relief, he declared they were historic.

He patted the new, polished bell awaiting its blessing from his future father-in-law, and it ascended into the belfry later in the day.

'Anonymous benefactor, wouldn't you know,' he said, watching the foundrymen load the old bell onto a wheeled trolley.

'Yes, serendipitous,' I replied. 'I hear the lightning rod and earthing bolts got their first proper test last week?'

'A veritable St Elmo's fire,' he said, turning with a look of unusual seriousness. 'No damage to the spire, and no sign of our playful spirit for six months.'

'That is a relief.' I changed the subject. 'Eleanor says you have set up a small studio inside your rebuilt outhouse?'

'Yes,' he said, breaking into a smile. 'Ellie calls it *The Folly*. Apt under the circumstances, don't you think?'

I grinned, amused by the inside joke, and I observed him pull out an envelope from his bag nearby.

'I mentioned that the vicar let me scour his library for you?' he said.

'Yes, though I'd quite forgotten about asking him on the night when we...'

Maxwell nodded and urged me to go no further.

'I needed to tell you in person; I didn't want Eleanor finding out,' he said.

'About what?' I said.

'Well, it turns out that the journal in my possession was the copy. The original is gathering dust on the vicar's library shelf.'

I glanced at the blank envelope being offered.

'You've read the undamaged entry? It exists?' I said.

'Yes, considering what it contains,' he whispered, 'I tore it from the original; he'll never know.'

'You could have just copied it?' I said, being a lover of old things, especially books.

'I never want the story to fall into the wrong hands again; the wrong, curious type of hands. If there was something in our weathercock, then there might be something in others.'

'Read it on your way home; it will explain a thing or two.' He shuffled, and seemed reticent to continue. 'I wonder, in hindsight, if it was the right course of action, setting fire to the outhouse, I mean.'

'I've been thinking on that myself, but what's done is done,' I said, putting the envelope into my breast pocket. 'Anyway, it seems you've impressed the vicar enough to win her hand.'

He pressed my shoulder and left me looking at the new bell. I squatted down and ran my fingers over the inscription, a gift to me from Maxwell in his unbreakable assertion that I was the benefactor. He had paid for its addition from his modest savings, and I was most touched by it.

For thou hast been a shelter for me, and a strong tower from the enemy. Psalm 61:3

I heard my old friend chatting with the foundrymen as I looked up at the roof of the ringing chamber beneath the belfry.

'Amen to that, my friend,' I said, 'amen.'

I RETURNED TO LONDON BY TRAIN THAT AFTERNOON AND was eager to learn what the journal page contained. I waited for the ticket inspector to leave and opened the envelope and unfolded the paper contents. It was complete, but also included diagrams, sketches and other inclusions, not seen in the entry that Maxwell had inherited. I believe that Maxwell's folios are mere drafts rather than copies from this book.

Just outside Windsor, a shaft of sunlight illuminated the page in my lap, and I read what it contained.

An account of the strange incidents and occurrences in the last week of September 1898, as witnessed by Richard Deveral, tower-warden of St Luke's, and by other notable people of the town.

We removed the medieval weathervane and cock from the spire on Holy Cross Day. The recent gales and centuries of service have rendered the noble artefact a hazard to all that worshipped below. The steeplejack delivered the fragile and rusted cardinal points, the sphere pedestal, and the mythical serpent-like creature that sat upon it. I sought out the blacksmith at the local inn, and he concluded that the metalwork was beyond repair. We agreed on a price for an exact copy, and the vicar has written to the Bishop asking for funds to accommodate him. It will be of the highest and most exact craftsmanship and, God willing, will last for centuries to come.

The hollow sphere broke in two with our rough handling at the inn, and curious ash spilt out, followed most urgently by something else. A sudden and invisible force leapt about the room before breaking out through the parlour window, but not before several unsuccessful attempts to escape by the chimney and door. The landlord and blacksmith have attested upon their oath that this was the order of things. I swept up the mess from the table and returned to the house, leaving the metalwork with the blacksmith. Closer examination revealed the contents to be minor pieces of bone and dust mixed with dark flakes of centuries-old rust; the fragments are charred or crematory in origin. I interred them within a small casket of my construction, fabricated from reliquary hardwoods the vicar bought from the Holy Land. The casket now resides securely within the tower, but the creature or spirit has made many appearances, attracted to what I presume to be its mortal remains or those of its kin.

When the bells are rung, the creature migrates to the belfry from far afield, to settle and slumber, as if in serene contentment. The landlord's son and I, in the charade of making some slight adjustment to the ringing wheel of the treble bell, lured the unruly creature beneath the propped tenor bell with the box of debris as bait. We called down for the ringers to begin their quarter peal, and the noise was deafening. The creature thrashed about within the bell until the ringing affected its state, and it became still. The bells swung wildly, and we had very little room to knock away the prop, imprisoning it beneath the massive bell. When we assured ourselves the thing was quiet, I tilted the bell back, and saw the faint outline of its small and coiled form in the dust; it is most assuredly the creature from the weathercock. Crossing myself, I picked up the scaly thing before placing it into the casket. It now sleeps, out of mischief, but assuredly continuing its protective work for the tower, and I note the position for those of you who come after.

I dare not open it again, not even to entomb it back in its rightful place on the steeple. The blacksmith will not entertain working on it for fear of injuring the creature or himself. What have we done?

It appears benign, and the records attest that the spire has never in recorded history been struck by lightning or endured any misadventure. The simple beliefs of the area ascribe a beneficial or guardian spirit to reside even within the simplest of weathercocks, and I am of the mind that these superstitions may have some basis in truth and that the thing is a shield against tempests and storms. It has a degree of physical form and scratches most unsettlingly in the belfry above, causing disquiet and talk of vermin amongst the congregation who are blessedly ignorant of its origin or nature.

God bless the tower and all those who ring within it.

R.D.

THE LAST LAUGH

There is no seaside town in England that can successfully support two Punch and Judy shows, and the sea-gulled seafront at Carston is no exception. It is a little place, with a pier that strides over the tide, resting on the pebbled shore and laurels of its Edwardian heyday. There is insufficient room in the small resort for more than one of anything if one genuinely wishes to make a living. There are, as this story will relate, no longer any such diversions at Carston, to its credit.

The two rival Punch and Judy men (or 'professors' to give them their Victorian formalities) used to entertain at opposite ends of the promenade before the tragic events of last year. The pier was a prime location but was often too windy for the red and white striped booths to withstand. It was also challenging to make out the squeaking Mr Punch and his cast over the roar of wind and surf, so it marked a mid-point, or no-man's-land between the two entertainers. Both shows were lively in distinct ways and took advantage of the brief, but busy, summer season on the east coast. Mr Dewhurst, the older of the professors, performed a family-friendly show.

The younger Mr Galton, the newcomer who had arrived the previous spring, was a purist and insisted on using the full menagerie of animals, ghosts and Mr Punch's penchant for abuse and violence. The latter's act was a profoundly unsettling performance, and not one for children, which may explain the general lack of success compared with the comical slapstick of Mr Dewhurst's show, a quarter of a mile away. One could visit both acts and come away with a unique perspective, though one Punch and Judy show is enough for anyone.

They observed mutual respect for timings out of necessity. The warm-hearted and retired Mr Dewhurst had reached out to encourage the recent arrival, with constructive criticism of the adult-orientated performance. The younger Mr Galton did not return the compliment and preferred to look upon his rival's act as a crass and perverted version of the true seventeenth-century morality play. Galton would squat on the pitch that offered the most passing traffic, but much to his annoyance, Dewhurst's more popular show always drew the bigger crowds.

Galton detested his rival and his performance. He was also in broad contempt of the very paying holidaymakers on whom he relied for his income. These tourists had made several complaints about the adult content of his act, forcing the council to issue a warning about the explicit nature of his performance. Children were left in tears from the ghoulish and violent aspects of Galton's show. Within the uncensored act, Mr Punch regularly fed his baby into the sausage machine, much to the wailing and weeping of his domestically abused wife, Judy. Her hook-nosed husband then used the slapstick to thrash her to within an inch of her wooden life, with the brutality lasting far beyond what good taste would usually allow for. Many disgusted holidaymakers typically made off at this point. A most unsettling and garishly painted devil later arrived with a frightening hangman to whisk the dreadful Mr Punch off to hell, out of sight below the stage. Still, the tortured squeaks of the puppet, issuing from the swazzle in the roof of Galton's mouth, left little to the imagination. The children and parents, none of whom had slept for days following Galton's performances, had complained to the tourist information centre. This show was not at all like the fun and friendly version they had visited further along the seafront, and they called for action.

The council insisted on a reduction in the show's depiction of abuse and gore, much to Galton's annoyance. He never knew who from the committee might watch the show, so he bided his time and complied. Profits were down, and he blamed everyone but himself for this. Galton also knew his high art played second fiddle to the commercial blandness on offer along the promenade, and it festered inside him.

Dewhurst was oblivious to the feelings of the younger professor, who watched and seethed from a lonely bench near his rival's booth. The children screamed with laughter, calling out 'Behind you!' to warn the benign version of Mr Punch of the threat posed by the comical and rather camp crocodile.

'*That's the way to do it!*' squeaked Dewhurst, as a single light blow despatched the farcical reptile. The children roared and applauded.

Galton was jealous of his rival's success, if not of the act. He was also envious of the puppets themselves. They were intricately carved, and of immense age; he scorned Dewhurst for creating so much happiness with valuable antiques when his act would benefit much more from their use. Galton's cast was from the late forties, mere imitations.

How he longed to get his hands into those antiques; that's what his act needed.

There were times when Dewhurst never set up, because of hospital appointments for his weak heart or to manage his bees in the local churchyard. His honey was legendary and prized for its purity. Galton hated bees, being allergic to insect bites and stings, but he capitalised mercilessly on the good fortune of those days. He relished the time when his petty lord of misrule commanded the promenade from the lower car park to the upper cliff-top. The public could then truly see what a real Punch and Judy show should be.

Galton fantasised of using those valuable puppets to super-charge his act. He would care for them better than the old duffer and become legendary, like the Italian founding fathers. He would travel far away from the idiotic day-trippers and local enforcement officers of the seafront, to perform across the country, perhaps even the world. The entire art form would blossom in a glorious revival, all thanks to Professor Galton, keeper and defender of the highest and noble Punch and Judy tradition.

There came a day of intense heat, coinciding, for once, with a bank holiday weekend. Sleepy Carston awoke and teemed with people from the nearby towns, eager to spend and enjoy themselves before the final plunge into autumn. Galton dripped with sweat, cocooned in his booth. There was a large crowd waiting for the macabre performance to begin, and he guzzled from a large bottle of lukewarm water. He started with the scarlet-cheeked Mr Punch, in charge of the baby from the long-suffering Judy. Her painted face was flaked from the beatings she then endured at the hands of her chaotic and coercive husband. Mr Plod, the policeman puppet, arrived to arrest the anti-hero but was despatched to his grave by the great slapstick that Mr Punch wielded with ferocity.

Galton resisted the urge to wipe his brow and wondered how his annoying rival was coping within the stifling heat. Three shows a day, and this was the last. Galton continued, exhausted, but revelling still in the performance. Throwing caution to the wind, he moved into his original and unadulterated production. They deserved to see the full show, the glorious and terrifying violence, and the range of his talents.

Sod the political correctness.

Punch turned the baby into sausages and fed them to Toby the dog, who then endured such animal cruelty as to send off the first of the parents. A sinister crocodile ate the puppet of the blind man and the bloodied version of his wife, setting off a child who wailed and called for its mother. Galton continued, undaunted, in the sweatbox that surrounded him. The hangman arrived, and the puppet danced at the end of a rope to Galton's cackling accompaniment. The fearsome devil dragged him into hell, dismembering him with a shriek before the legless Mr Punch gained the upper hand, literally. Punch lopped off the head of the demonic puppet with such force that it flew out into the thinning crowd. Galton heard a shrill cry of alarm from the unfortunate catcher. He was close to the finale and near to passing out. Punch returned from the fiery pits of the underworld, resurrected and whole. He was victorious against the forces of evil, who proved powerless to stop the abuse and the killings.

The curtains drew, and there was sparse and muted applause from outside, mostly out of British politeness than for any genuine appreciation. Galton stuck his head out at the back of the tent and breathed in the refreshing air. The honesty box was light for such a sizeable crowd, and he considered giving them a piece of his mind for being so cheap in front of such a theatrical performance. They walked away, shaking their heads, barely able to process what they had just witnessed. They sauntered in the pier's direction and towards his rival.

Dripping with sweat, Galton stretched his legs and went in search of something cold to drink. He passed the pier and saw the crowd of animated children at Dewhurst's booth shouting 'Behind you!' as the supporting characters got the better of his Mr Punch and morality returned, setting the world to rights. Despite the success of Dewhurst's performance, it was clear he was flagging. The climax of the show approached, and Galton smiled at the thought of the older man suffering in his plastic-covered booth, fluffing his lines and struggling to keep the puppets in the air. Galton saw his rival's arms droop as if desperate for the play to finish. Dewhurst's hurried dialogue became weak and almost inaudible as the performance came to an abrupt end with the hasty drawing of the stage curtains.

The crowd erupted into applause, despite the rapid conclusion, and they fed clinks of loose change into the box at the booth's side. There was a brief shudder from within, and then all was still. The crowd dispersed and immersed themselves in shade and suntan lotion.

Galton guzzled several ice-cold lemonades and wandered closer to Dewhurst's booth. There was no sign of the older man posing for pictures with the children, as he usually did after the show. He made his way to the back and parted the striped slit to see the purple-faced professor, slumped, with eyes dilated, and struggling to breathe. On his lap lay several of the beautiful and antique puppets, and his right hand clutched the cord of the drawn curtain. Dewhurst recognised the younger man and moaned, pointing with the Mr Punch on his right hand to a pillbox by his feet. Galton stared back and then jealously at the puppets strewn backstage. Dewhurst moaned again, realising Galton was not there to help him.

Galton removed his head from the booth and looked back and forth. A few tourists lay on the grass some distance away, licking ice creams and absorbed in talk. Two children fished for crabs in the middle of the pier and did not look over.

The pitch was devoid of anyone witnessing the tragedy playing out behind the curtain and vacant of anyone who had noticed the younger man's visit to the booth. Galton's blood coursed and pounded in his head as he turned and left the older man to die, stifling and alone.

Galton meandered around the promenade, and he thought on the man's last breaths, but he consoled himself with the beautiful puppets and the monopoly he would enjoy. He hadn't killed the man, he told himself. The silly old fool should have had his pills closer to hand and not performed during the hottest day of the year.

The thrill did not leave him as he reached his booth, and he planned how to get the puppet set of his dreams from Dewhurst, who lay dying only five hundred yards away.

He waited and watched for over an hour as the seafront cleared, staring out from his small stage. Dewhurst's far away booth remained quiet and still. Adrenaline coursed through his veins as he thrust his puppets into a rucksack and walked back towards the opportunity of his lifetime. He slowed his pace and tried to slow his breathing as he approached the striped tent. He took a last look around and darted into the confined space of Dewhurst's booth. Galton took out his puppets and exchanged them for the set of his heart's desire. His hands trembled as he pulled the Punch from Dewhurst's clammy and cold hand. There was a twitch from the body at his feet, and Galton started in alarm. The wide eyes of the older man remained open as he wheezed out his last breath.

'*Beeeeeeez...*'

Galton zipped his rucksack closed and peered out of the slit. He waited for a couple to pass and slipped out unseen, back to his pitch, shivering with exhilaration. The gleeful voice of Mr Punch echoed in his mind.

Now that's the way to do it!

He packed up his booth and emptied the payment box of

its meagre contents. Taking one last look at Dewhurst's distant mausoleum, he drove out of the car park and home to examine his newly gained treasures.

He got in and tried on the puppets. They were marvellous, and now in the right hands, literally. He imagined how much these would have cost him or other aficionados at auction; the Mr Punch alone was worth thousands of pounds. The carvings were exquisite but, in the fading light of his compact kitchen, somehow gothic, fantastical and otherworldly. They had a beauty and a feeling, unlike his tatty old imitations that lay on Dewhurst's lap. He shot a glance at the devil he had exchanged and had an uncomfortable feeling of guilt, having left the older man to his gasping fate. Galton threw a cushion over the puppet and stood up as an ambulance raced by on its way to the seafront.

They had found the body.

He panicked, and fear of discovery rose in his chest. Would they know the puppets had been switched? No, surely not.

Dewhurst had died a natural death brought on by the extraordinary heat. That would be the verdict. He relaxed, but anxiety returned when he realised his swazzle was missing. The kazoo-like device that created the screeching vocabulary of Mr Punch was not in its usual place. He became anxious when he could not discover it in the car, or the rucksack.

Had it fallen out at the booth, or with Dewhurst? Would the police even know what it was? Without it, he couldn't work efficiently and would have to rely on his voice. He would buy a replacement, and then if he laid low for a few days, people would think he was paying his respects.

But would it be better for him to turn up tomorrow because he shouldn't know the man was dead, should he?

The circular reasoning and questions continued all night, and he rose at dawn, dishevelled and weary.

GALTON HEARD THE NEWS ON THE RADIO AS HE DROVE TO the seafront. William Dewhurst, a bachelor with no next of kin, had been found dead by a passing drunk who had gone into the booth to shelter for the night. Dewhurst had likely suffered a heart attack triggered by overwork and heat exhaustion. He had been donating his fees to the local church, and the vicar described him as a lovely, kind, and generous soul whose honey was famous throughout the district. Many lamented the fate of the man and his bees.

Galton set up his booth and then wandered over to the spot where a small bunch of flowers lay. He stooped to read the card.

RIP The best Punch and Judy show in Carston.

He scowled and returned to his pitch, passing several of the townsfolk who had turned out to pay their respects at the site of Dewhurst's final performance.

Galton set out his board and feigned dignity by only performing once in respect for his fallen comrade. A single show, with feelings running high, could be very profitable. He wrote '*Proceeds to the church spire*' in all but illegible script at the base of the show board and decided to perform one of the older man's routines. He would spice it up with the crocodile he had gained and use the new puppets and one or two of his existing dolls. He began rehearsing at once, much to the disdain of passing folk who thought it inappropriate for Galton to be working at all.

Midday approached, and a modest crowd formed in a sombre mood. Word had got about that Dewhurst had died 'on stage' and Galton had arranged a show in tribute. He came out front and began the presentation, with honeyed words of affection for the death of a magnificent Punch and Judy man. He hoped that his unique performance would offer some comfort and a chance for all present to contribute towards the fund closest to the older man's heart. The vicar was busy elsewhere, and all the faces seemed to be holiday-makers who would not have the foggiest what would happen to the money. Wasps and bees buzzed by, attracted by the ice-cream cornets of cross-legged children, and the bright colours of the booth.

GALTON PARTED THE FLAPS AND ENTERED THE CONFINED space, putting on the glove puppets. Something bit several times into his right hand, and he cried out in pain. A wasp? He tried to remove the puppet, but his swelling hand prevented him from doing so. Mr Punch looked down at his crouching form and squeaked in laughter from his hand. Galton panicked, trying to remove the stinging thing within and reaching for his EpiPen to prevent the anaphylactic shock from his severe allergy. The puppet continued to squeak, and Galton realised in horror that it was not his voice creating the sound. He had no swazzle, and the voice at the end of his arm cackled with glee. His arms would not respond and rigidly extended into the stage area.

'*That's the way to do it!*' cried Punch. '*Beeeeeeez...*'

Galton looked up in horror at the red-cheeked face of the demonic Mr Punch. It mirrored the burning face of Dewhurst, desperate for aid, and Galton thrashed about wildly, trying to dislodge it. The crocodile on his left hand constricted around his wrist, preventing him from picking up and administering the life-saving injection. He felt a burning cold rapidly infect his veins on its way to his heart. He screamed for mercy. At the same time, the reptile thrust itself up into the theatre to join the Mr Punch with a life of its own.

From outside, the performance appeared to be in terrible taste. There was a lot of thrashing and violent interplay between the two figures on display. Mr Punch jerked and squeaked maniacally, occasionally stopping to batter the crocodile who screamed in Galton's normal voice for mercy. The onlookers grew restless and disbanded, uncomfortable with the heinous wails and blood-curdling screams from within the tent. The show was disturbing, and not in the slightest entertaining.

Galton heard the boos from many of the departing crowd, any of whom could save him. He tried to roll backwards out of the booth, but he found it firmly toggled shut and then began to lose consciousness.

The things on his hands had other plans for him.

Satisfied the pitch was clear, the puppets turned to look down in vengeance and sank below the stage-line. Something terrible beneath Galton's feet tugged at the curtain cord, and the booth's interior descended into a red shadow. The fire crept into his chest, and he convulsed into shock and inevitable coma. The last thing he saw was the grinning red faces of Dewhurst's puppets cascading, biting and beating down onto his slumping form. Mr Punch produced the missing swazzle and rammed it deep into the open mouth, causing the last expulsion of squeaking terror before Galton's heart stopped.

His last performance was over.

The seafront of Carston came to terms with the death of the other Punch and Judy man, many hours later. Anaphylaxis was the verdict of the coroner, brought on by exposure to a potent allergen. The police noted that the EpiPen remained unused and nearby, mirroring the tragedy of Dewhurst's proximity to his life-saving medicine. What they could not fathom were the bite marks and severe bruising, likely caused by a blunt instrument at or around the time of death. The specialists had to remove the puppets surgically from what remained of Galton's stumps, but what had caused the injuries was a mystery. That the crocodile puppet was bloodied and missing several of its teeth did not seem relevant.

Two months later, a police auction failed to sell the puppets, or the booths and paraphernalia. News had spread, and nothing stops a sale like superstition or the taint of bad luck. You will find the top half of Dewhurst's Mr Punch grinning eternally from a cultural museum in the West Country; the trouble-maker no longer able to wield his slapstick. Many other figures, partly damaged, ended up in charity shops.

I warn you against any purchase should you discover them.

The small resort of Carston is now an altogether quieter place and continues to decline into obscurity. The promenade is now free from the sound of the swazzle, silent in all but the seabirds and the slumbering shore.

BELOVED

The trouble with being immortal is that mealtimes become rather dull once you have eaten everything you can hunt, a thousand times. Food becomes a basic necessity rather than the fulfilment of desire when the feathered or whiskered prey you rely upon make up much of your diet.

Rats were plentiful during the plague, and Lundi took to the meat with trepidation. The scratching, squeaking things always frightened her.

Before the changing.

She had woken one night in her wooden cot, stuffed with straw, to discover a whiskered terror on her chest. She screamed for her mother, and comfort came swiftly from the next room.

Now it was the rat's turn to scream as Lundi hunted them.

'*When the plague comes to the village, you had better hide!*' the wise woman warned, '*Play like beasts, here in the wood and learn to escape and endure. Play and hunt in the Sperrow until I return, or forever if I don't.*'

In the beginning, the urge to hunt was so strong that fighting against it led to severe stress and intense hunger.

Giving in to the new instinct was a tremendous relief, and Lundi only considered the raw vermin later, when she regurgitated the meal in revulsion. A memory from her former existence, now vague and fleeting, emphasised that such things were not good to eat.

She was born on a Monday, in the reign of old King Henry, and was the only surviving child of the village blacksmith. Her family had succumbed quickly to the plague, but she outlived them by centuries.

She was a pretty child at eight years old, even with the grub and grime of Medieval England. The simple country life could not hide her flaming hair, green eyes and freckled skin. Her actual name was long forgotten, but Lundi didn't need it after the magical transformation.

'Monday's child is fair of face,' said the woman, *'You are both blessed and cursed to live in such times. Fated to be born and die on the same day.'*

People drifted through the overgrown lanes, and the distant circling of crows heralded the Black Death in the village. Her playmates, of comparable age, lost their families too and they foraged together along the riverbank and the dark woodland edge.

They learned not to go into the Sperrow, a vast area of woodland stretching from the river to the far downs. Superstition held that something ancient lurked within, independent of human morality. Benign, but fae; something belonging to the old days, which was best left alone and undisturbed. When children strayed in, some never came out.

Hunger and necessity forced them inside. The boys made fires and camps to keep warm while the girls caught pigeon and gathered berries. The constables burned down their homes to the ground to control the spread of the disease, cleansing from existence the life they once knew. Lundi thought it strange that something so simple as fire could destroy what God had sent as a punishment for man's wickedness.

She was the first to come upon the wise woman, deep in the Sperrow. Chasing a rabbit, she followed the drifting smoke of a distant fire to a small clearing. Hunger made her curious but wary.

'Come closer, child,' said the wise woman, emerging from the small wooden hut, ringed with seven enormous stones.

Lundi had never seen such a venerable face. Her grandmother had died at forty, and she thought that to be old.

'Do you like sweet rolls?' said the woman, beckoning her forward. She disappeared back into the hut and emerged with a covered basket. The smell of freshly baked cakes rose from the carrier. 'Take them for the others, if you don't.'

The woman backed away, and Lundi shuffled forward to collect the offering.

'Do not go back to the village,' said the woman, 'death is still there. Come back tomorrow and bring another.'

Lundi returned with the oldest of the children. The son of the thatcher, he was a sturdy lad and protective of his new wards. He insisted on seeing the strange woman to assess the danger and further investigate the prospects for food.

In the coming days, they all came for the sweet rolls and the stories. The woman sat on an old tree stump and lightened the dark, uncertain days. The plague would come searching for them, she warned, and no-one was safe from its deadly glance. Only those who were small and stealthy, like a cat, could elude its pestilent gaze. She offered a choice. Live forever, transformed, but free to play and hunt for eternity. Death was merely a possibility if they did not hide from the world on the day of their birth. It was a certainty if they remained as they were.

The thatcher's son changed first, keen to show his courage, but not believing that anything unusual would happen. Born on a Saturday, he was warned to hide on that day of the week lest misadventure take him and revert him lifeless and cold to the form of his birth.

'Saturday's child will work hard for his living,' the woman said, as the thatcher's son rolled and frolicked in his unfamiliar form. He shot up a tree and purred at them all below.

The younger children fled, only venturing back later to peer through the brambles at the clearing's edge. Lundi remained to play and stroke the kitten who did not appear to be in any distress. The former playmate rejoiced in his newfound agility, and Lundi marvelled at his foaming blue and mossy green coloured eyes. There was recognition there, teeming with joy and encouragement to join him.

She turned, eager for the others.

'They will return,' said the woman, glancing over at the mass of thorny overgrowth, 'You must lead them now, to change or stay as they are. Your choice will be the last, for now.'

The children returned meekly, then changed and endured, each in turn warned about venturing abroad on the days of their birth. After many days of searching, Lundi led the thin, quiet boy back from his hiding place in the meadow. The old woman held him long in her gaze as though perceiving something profound and confident in his future.

'Far to go, young master, hide now from each Thursday and live forever!'

Lundi changed shortly after; it was the end of sweet rolls or any appetite for them.

The wise woman comforted and nurtured the new kittens until they could fend for themselves. They grew strong and keen, revelling in each other's company whenever they encountered a former playmate. Further and further afield, they wandered and less often did they visit each other or the clearing. Never did seven appear at once. They heeded the wise woman's warning and there was always one, secret and hidden, depending on the day of the week.

When Lundi returned months later, she found the deserted hut dilapidated and the ring of seven stones overgrown with flowering bindweed. It was time to forge a life alone, and eternally, six days a week.

The plague did finally relent, and the land and its people recovered until civil war broke out. Families, divided by King and Parliament, turned on each other. A dreadful battle took place in the fields nearby. Lundi heard the first loud cannon mark its bloody beginning, followed by the screams and agony of the dying in the dry September grass. Men fleeing from the battle escaped into the Sperrow and did not come out. Lundi waited several days before venturing into the meadow to hunt, to discover the rats preying on the exposed soldiers. She caught only birds then until the first snows came; a white blanket to cover the memory of the 'Red Field', as it became known ever after.

Rarely did she trust in the company of people, but an occasional child straying close to the Sperrow might be worth investigating if they had a treat or two.

She would come across the other siblings from time to time, a fellowship that was breakable only by death. She became less sure of the reason behind the feelings of kinship but had joy in seeing them, specifically the quiet, ragged-looking brother with emerald and amber eyes. In the century that followed, she saw them less and less; the tall Saturday child and her old black-haired playmate, born on a Friday, she never saw again.

Time wore on but had little effect on Lundi. She hid every Monday in a disused owl's hole, high in a venerable oak. People came and went, and morsel stealing children grew up and had children of their own. A grand Palladian mansion rose from the grassy ruins of the village and a duke established a pleasure park to envelop it. Lundi gazed down at her reflection in the newly created lake, gouged out of the thick clay by a hundred wooden spades. Her coloured chartreuse and opal eyes stared back, trying to recall some memory of the taste of sweet rolls over the lingering freshly eaten pheasant.

One summer, a youthful and richly dressed girl took to her most affectionately. Driven part way in a carriage with a chaperone, she would walk to the lake edge to view the estate and the newly installed follies. The beautiful ginger and cream cat bewitched the girl, and she longed to be in Lundi's company as she slept on the sun-baked stones of the water's edge. The slow path to trust began, mouthful by mouthful, lasting the long life of Belladonna Hargreaves.

Lundi enjoyed many exquisite delicacies, filched by her new and eager to please patron. Belladonna left the food on a patterned handkerchief, six days a week, and called out to her, using an unfamiliar name. The food was left closer and closer to the house every time. Her father indulged his daughter's every whim and allowed the handsome, but feral creature finally into the house, despite several expensive porcelain vases knocked over from finely worked and scratched side tables.

Belladonna would yearn and call out in anguish for the cat that disappeared every Monday. Lundi would hear her distantly calling, over the sound of her rumbling stomach, safe and dark in the ancient tree. Tuesday was always a joyful meeting, and both parties got used to the arrangement.

The girl grew into an exceptional beauty, and the duke presented her at court, as was the custom. He hoped to secure a profitable and worthy suitor now that his daughter was eighteen years of age, and commissioned a magnificent portrait for her birthday. She only consented to sit for lengthy periods providing the cat could share in her tedious boredom.

No-one told the artist to omit the animal, and there was talk of non-payment when her father first stared in horror at his folly. There was his oil-painted daughter, in beautiful blue silk, a secondary figure in a scene dominated by the cat. Belladonna jumped with joy and held her father so tightly that he had to pay the artist in full.

Lundi, now tamed, enjoyed every comfort imaginable. The preceding decades had been bleak and the child, now married, had been her ticket out of harsh times, at least while she lived.

Decades later, Belladonna inherited the estate on the death of her husband. She took to sitting and dozing in the fireside chair while Lundi considered the two women in the room that bore the same name. The first was above the mantelpiece, painted long ago. A youthful woman with smooth pale skin smiled back, with the cat alongside on a table doing its very best to imitate her. The second lay reposed beneath Lundi's furry body, the same woman, but now weary and arthritic. Unable to ride or climb the grand stairs, Belladonna took a keen interest in the new steam-powered age, which promised advances for the estate and its workers.

Belladonna lived to a marvellous age for the time, and Lundi had survived all but unchanged. Her feline beauty continued to attract attention and admiration even as her mistress aged and withered. When the widow died at eighty-two, they laid her coffin beneath the portrait, and people suddenly noticed an odd thing.

'Surely not the same cat?' said the footman, pointing to Lundi in the portrait and then back to the cat, mournfully in repose on the windowsill.

'Well, I've been here for over thirty years, and my mother says it was here when she was a maid. We've never known another, not with those eyes,' said the cook.

197

Gossip about the cat's extreme age got out, and crowds came by to see it and the house during the sale of the contents. The only surviving heir, a distant cousin who farmed in the Americas, became the beneficiary but never visited and the house fell into decay. It was the former gardener who settled the affair by making up Lundi's favourite meal one evening before caging her. He had played with her, long ago before entering service, and it broke his heart to betray her and see her yowling and scratching at the locked basket. He knew that something was not right with the natural order of things. The cat would end up as a dreadful curiosity or worse if it remained.

He carried her to a gypsy camped in the woods who held more positive and understanding superstitions about owning a cat with strange eyes, and one that did not seem to age. The gardener stroked her until she calmed down and cried the whole three miles walk back, empty-handed to the servant's cottages.

The tale of the strange cat died down with her disappearance, and they never saw Belladonna's beloved again. She still looks out, proudly and eternally, from a gallery far away.

There is one other, a ragged cat with green and amber eyes, who still remembers her to this day; he will often roam far and wide in search of her. When he is not hiding from Thursday, he checks at every old oak tree near the present children's hospice, built on the edge of Sparrow Wood.

But only, of course, on Mondays.

TWO LEFT FEET

Jess's dance studio was the perfect room to hold the viewing of the coffin. There was an irony in having her boyfriend's body in the ample open space, usually so full of movement and vigour. Here he lay, amongst his medical colleagues, in the one place he had most feared to tread when alive, oblivious to family and friends who consoled the love of his life in her bottomless grief.

'How did he die?' asked a distant cousin.

'Something he caught at the hospital where he worked,' replied a closer cousin. 'They don't say exactly what, but it was quick. He was a lovely lad and was planning to move into her flat above the studio. Those are his bits and bobs over there, next to the sandwiches and cakes for the wake.' The relation pointed to a stack of boxes and sheet-covered objects in the corner.

One item stood tall and ghostlike, a static human form draped in a substantial white cloth. It remained motionless as the mourners and coffin departed for the funeral, leaving it solitary and silent, staring out at its shrouded reflection in the mirrored wall opposite.

They returned two hours later, and Jess was dry from tears. She could barely recall the service, as she concentrated on defending her composure against fresh waves of sorrow. Chris's younger brother, Will, had given the eulogy and he had held her tightly throughout the lowering of the coffin. She was his sister in all but name and had been around as long as he could remember. Chris had confided to Will that he would ask Jess to marry him after graduating as a doctor, and he would need a best man. Will sobbed with the foreknowledge that he would keep it secret, to prevent further sadness, until the day when, strangely, she would ask him about it.

The mourners left. Sylvia, the part-time help and Jess's former dance teacher, remained to sweep away the event and cling-film the food. She watched as her brightest pupil, withered and burdened by tragic circumstance, drew apart the gauze privacy curtains and opened the sash windows to let in the evening's last rays of sunshine. The breeze caught the light fabric, and a beam of spring sunlight travelled across the floor to illuminate the tall shrouded object.

Jess wandered over and stared at the foreign and yet familiar item.

'Is that one of Chris's things?' asked Sylvia, desperate to comfort her young protégé.

'Yes,' said Jess, distantly. 'It's Mr Bone-Jangles.'

'Mr who?'

Jess smiled for the first time since the fateful day she had received news from the hospital.

'Chris's medical skeleton,' she said, tugging at the covering, and setting the plastic bones rattling like a humanoid bead curtain suspended from its metal stand.

'Oh, my dear thing,' said Sylvia, 'do you think you should have this in the apartment at a time like this?'

'I said the same myself,' said Jess, staring into its eye sockets.

'I told Chris it would be 'over my dead body' that he brought it to live with us. He told me it would only be until he got a practice of his own. I don't think I have the heart to throw him out now; Chris thought a lot of him.' She remembered the Valentine's Day surprise when he had sneaked out early, leaving the skeleton with a red rose in its mouth and a chocolate heart embedded in its chest. She had discovered it when she prepared the room for the first dance student of the morning.

'Well, look at its feet,' said Sylvia. 'It doesn't look like Mr Bone-Jangles has a matching pair.'

A medical skeleton was an expensive item, except on rare occasions when damaged or incomplete versions came with a substantial discount.

Jess smiled again, broadly and warmly. 'He has two left feet, just like Chris. Ironic, isn't it? Chris couldn't dance and only humoured me when I tried to teach him. It took me weeks to get over the bruises from the foxtrot.' She collected the sheet and covered the skeleton. 'I think I'll keep him for now, at least until we reopen.'

'Very good, dear,' said Sylvia. 'Have you given thought to that yet?'

Jess had given plenty of thought to the reopening of the small, but profitable, business. Every time, a little voice cried out inside, '*Not yet. It's too early.*'

'Soon,' she replied, helping Sylvia with her coat. 'I need to get my head straight first, you understand?'

Sylvia nodded and headed for the door. 'Well, I'll be here in the morning anyway to finish up and take any calls. You know where I am if you need me.'

'Thanks for everything, Sylvia,' said Jess, 'and thanks for not pressing about the church thing. I know it's important to you, but I need to get over this myself.'

'We are always here if you need us,' said Sylvia, as she

made her way to the Wednesday meeting at the Spiritualist centre.

Jess waited for silence to return, and she stared at herself in the mirrored wall. The wind billowed the curtain and moved the skeleton's sheet.

'*Soon...*' came a whisper, or was it an echo?

She closed the window and took off her shoes. She softly padded over to the sound booth, switched on the speakers and put on the track that was Chris's favourite. Jess loosened her clothing as the acoustic guitar kicked in.

The song looped and she danced until her mascara streaked from the pouring rain of her tears.

THE STUDIO DID NOT REOPEN SOON, AND JESS SPIRALLED into gloom. Friends and family rallied, hopeful for a time before the grief took hold once again and she locked herself away.

The business dried up, and red letters appeared. Sylvia tried to encourage Jess to leave the apartment but had resorted to banging on the other side of the apartment door. She could not gain access until she threatened to call social services and Jess relented by allowing her in. The poor girl was in a mess; even the cat had given up and moved into the house opposite.

'I'm praying for you, Jess; we all are,' said Sylvia. 'God knows you miss him, but you have to make a start on the rest of your life; it's what Chris would have wanted.'

'Soon,' said Jess vacantly, wishing that even Sylvia would leave her be.

'I'll be back tomorrow to hold you to that,' said Sylvia. 'You need to get out, Jess, and eat something. How can you go on with black coffee and tinned fruit?'

'I promise, Sylvia,' said Jess, picking at her dressing gown. 'I just need a little more time.'

Jess closed the door quietly and heard Sylvia sob from beyond. Jess slunk down and gripped her knees, listening as her friend wiped her eyes and blew her nose on a handkerchief. Sylvia knelt and placed a hand on the door. Jess reached out her own, missing the touch of human contact but feeling guilty for the comfort it would bring.

It was a long hour before Sylvia got up and left. The studio phone rang from downstairs, which was unusual. The calls had gradually decreased and nearly stopped altogether, and Sylvia had diverted the rest to the answerphone. The ringing continued, well past any normal human behaviour, and she opened the door, calling out in case Sylvia might be downstairs.

There was no response, only the constant ringing of the bell. After ignoring it for twenty minutes, Jess crumbled and put on her comfortable black dance tee and pants, in case she encountered anyone on the stairs in the shared building. She unlocked the studio, slid across the dusty floor, and lifted the receiver.

'Hello?' she said. 'We're closed until further notice.'

'*You took your time, Jess, considering you've got nothing better to do,*' whispered the voice at the other end. It sounded remote.

Hearing her name mentioned spooked her; she was an attractive woman and was used to unwanted attention.

'Who is this?' she asked.

'*Who do you think?*' came the reply. '*Sylvia keeps bleating on about you at her meetings, and having seen you now, she's bloody right.*' The phone clicked, and the call was over, but the whisper came clearly from the room instead. '*You need to get over me; I can't move on either till you do.*'

Jess dropped the receiver. She looked around wildly, searching for the source of the sound.

'This is not funny, messing with me like this. Did Sylvia put you up to this at her church? You don't know what I'm going through!'

'*Oh yes I do,*' came the whisper from the corner of the room, '*except I don't wallow in tears and feel sorry for myself way beyond what is normal.*'

Jess choked. 'Chris?'

'*I've come back to say goodbye and do the only thing I never had the guts to do.*'

The covered skeleton briefly moved and settled, rattling the pieces of fake bone. Jess looked over at the closed window and back at the skeleton's feet swaying beneath the shroud.

'*Put my song on, then dance with me...*'

'With Mr Bone-Jangles?'

'*Well, it will be difficult holding on to a cloth for you, and the ghostly bedsheet look is so M. R. James, don't you think? Hurry, I've only got a brief time to say goodbye.*'

Jess shook as she programmed the player and switched on the music system.

She glanced across at the mirror to see the sheet withdraw and the skeleton's animated hands unhooking itself from the stand.

'*I always wanted to lose a few pounds, but this is ridiculous,*' said the skeleton, jaw unmoving but inhabited by the ghost of her beloved. '*Can you work with this?*'

She nodded and ran over to embrace the animated form. It put its arms around her, and she wept.

'*It's okay,*' said the ghost. '*I feel the same, but we both need closure. Hurry now; you must lead and watch my feet!*'

Jess withdrew and took one arm of the skeleton, wrapping it around her waist. She took the other and clasped it, swaying side to side before lightly leading her ghoulish partner through the steps of an Argentine tango. The socketed eyes stared blankly back, and she thought there was just the hint of a smile on the skeleton's face. The song played out and reached the last verse.

'Are you all right?' asked Jess.

'*Yes, but I need to know you will be too. You should make a go of this place and don't be afraid to live. You don't need my permission, you know?*' The skeleton disentangled itself and hobbled over to the dusty artificial display of flowers on the trophy cabinet. It rattled back to the centre of the room and knelt, offering the rose to Jess, who joined the skeleton on the floor.

'*Ask my brother about the secret he is keeping back from you; it will release him and bring you both peace, I hope.*' The song was ending.

'I don't understand,' said Jess. 'Why do you have to go?'

'*Because I love you, and I want you to go on without me.*' The skeleton leaned forwards and kissed her. For a fleeting moment, the face of her lover and best friend smiled back with the song's final chorus repeating to a murmur.

She held on to the form, sensing the end, as the skeleton wobbled and fell into her arms, lifeless and unmoving, despite her cries. The rose fell between the mismatched feet, and she cried for the last time. She sat cross-legged with the skeleton in her lap until moonlight peeped in through the window and bathed the makeshift sign for the original opening of the studio, twelve months before.

'*Opening Soon, beginners welcome.*'

'I UNDERSTAND YOU OFFER FINAL DANCE LESSONS WITH...' The man on the phone hesitated, searching in the awkward silence for the right words. 'The recently departed? Sylvia mentioned you at the meeting, and what happened to you.

I'm not sure if that makes sense or even if I should have troubled you.'

Jess got out her diary, still processing the idea that this could happen to someone else, three months after she had reopened the studio.

'It makes perfect sense,' she said, 'and it's no trouble. How does next Monday at 8 pm sound?'

'I can make that, but what about my wife? Will she know the time?'

Jess looked at the skeleton. It moved imperceptibly in the breeze from the open window.

'She'll know. Have either of you danced before, Mr...?' she asked, getting out her pen.

'Mr and Mrs Cartwright, and no, not really,' said the man. 'She always had two left feet.'

Our revels now are ended. These our actors,
As I foretold you, were all spirits, and
Are melted into air, into thin air...

Prospero, *The Tempest.*

GET EXCLUSIVE CONTENT

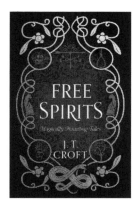

Thank you for reading *High Spirits*.

Building a relationship with my readers is the very best thing about writing. I send monthly newsletters with details on new releases, special offers and other news relating to my books.

Sign up to my readers' group at www.jtcroft.com or by scanning the QR code below, and I'll send you further stories in my collection, *Free Spirits*, exclusive to my reader's group– you can't get this anywhere else.

ALSO BY J. T. CROFT

Midnight's Treasury

A House of Bells

"Dead Brilliant"

★★★★★

"Well written. Fascinating and original"

★★★★★

"Beautifully dark and bittersweet"

★★★★★

ABOUT THE AUTHOR

J. T. Croft is the author of Gothic fiction, supernatural mystery and ghostly short stories.
For more information:
www.jtcroft.com

I hope you enjoyed reading this book as much as I loved writing it. If you did, I'd really appreciate you leaving me a quick review on whichever platform you prefer. Reviews are extremely helpful for any author, and even just a line or two can make a big difference. I'm independently published, so I rely on good folks like you spreading the word!

facebook.com/jtcroftauthor
twitter.com/jtcroftauthor
instagram.com/jtcroftauthor

AFTERWORD

The tales contained within this collection represent some of my earliest work. The ideas stretch back some forty years or so and are apologetically whimsical, fanciful and, by their very nature, deeply personal. I never had an imaginary friend or was visited by any form of spirit, benign or malevolent, but I have been fascinated by the idea of their interference for as long as I can remember.

This probably originates from my first experiences with Dickens' *A Christmas Carol*, which manages to emotionally tug its reader through darkness and light, within its intended social commentary narrative. He champions the vulnerable and the weak, and that resonates with me deeply. I think it is the greatest novella ever written.

There is often a 'What if?' question that kick-starts my frenzied attempt to capture my fleeting ideas on the page, and I always imagine them coming into the world unannounced like newborn stars from the giant dust cloud swirling around in my head. They always occur like a bolt of lightning when I am doing something completely abstract or to the contrary, and no amount of 'muse-hunting' for them has ever yielded better results than when they manifest of their own accord.

I include a brief history and my ramblings on each tale, partly out of self-indulgence, but mostly out of a deteriorating memory. I should like to remember how and why I created them, and maybe you will find them interesting. Like a father looking back at the earliest photos of his children, I should like to recall and relive the emotion that sparked them into being. I hope that your own experiences with them will be enhanced and not spoiled by my attempts to shine a light on their themes and background; it is, of course, the job of the writer to subtly convey his or her meaning, but the job of the reader to decide and interpret for themselves.

The short stories in this volume represent my best possible work at the time of writing (2020) and I ask readers of my future works to enjoy them for what they are: the genesis of my creative writing. I also apologise here, to my American readers, for the British English.

May creative spirits always be working with or through you.

J. T. Croft, 2020

ABOUT THE TALES

THE SPIRIT OF THE PLACE

This came fully formed like a bolt from the blue, one Sunday morning. By the evening it was complete, and the muse retired to bedlam. It has an *Alan Bennett* feel to it, if he wrote cosy supernatural, and may be influenced by the humour of '*The Canterville Ghost*' by Oscar Wilde.

It stems from a study on loneliness and the elderly. I was moved by my own writing for the first time in this tale, especially in the terrible 'letting go' of someone for their own good. Stewart Granger happened to be a favourite film star of my grandmother, and as I think it is my best short story, I dedicate it to her.

TYBURN'S SHADOW

Spectral highwaymen and dashing duels! This tale came quickly and forms part of a larger work in progress. It was a hoot to research, though the history of Tyburn Tree is not for the faint-hearted. Its dark themes enjoy a playfulness amongst the two protagonists coming to terms with their shared predicament, and I confess I am much more Tom than I am Flint.

THE MOST MAGNIFICENT MENKA

This tale came running for the bus as it was pulling out of the station. With editor deadlines looming, it banged on the door as I was driving and refused to leave me alone until I had exhausted myself over two days in telling it. I removed a tale to make way for its presence in the collection and it is my 'Gaiman-esque' inclusion.

I have walked many long-distance footpaths, but the Camino de Santiago in Southern France/Northern Spain is one of the oldest and the longest. I wondered about the travellers and the troubadours who plied their trade centuries ago, and the idea of a magic trick 'going awry' in superstitious times. It has an 'Ockham's razor' theme running through it, where the simplest explanation is the most likely, and staring the crowds of the show in the face. After all, who would expect a travelling stage magician of performing real magic?

THE DARK HEART

'The Dark Heart' started life as 'Simkin's Chair', and was my attempt at a *'Jamesian'* (M. R. James) tale. There may be elements of *'The Stalls of Barchester Cathedral'* by the aforementioned master of ghost stories, as well as my own public-school education.

There is always a Simkin, somewhere, and we must do our best to beat them, without 'beating' them.

The misericord in question is inspired by open-mouthed carvings of wyverns on the choir stalls at St Mary's Church, Fairford, Gloucestershire.

MY FELLOW MAN

I had been walking the yellow rape field near my home during the Covid-19 lockdown, listening to a podcast on financial independence. The world, and the markets, had gone into meltdown over the virus and the hosts of the show were offering their advice to those with investments. One host commented that no one could predict the future, certainly not market analysts. I stopped, dealing with the sudden appearance of the *What If?* spirit.

A time-traveller could make a fortune, and this story began as a science-fiction tale. Remnants still remain from this earlier concept before it morphed into something else entirely. It is at its core a story about friendship and the trusting of one's gut, despite a firm nudge in the right direction from something 'unknown'. The appearance of the smartly dressed man with a curious birthmark leaving the church is an intended 'Easter egg' to another much longer tale, yet to be fully developed. I like him enough to have faith in (and spend time on!) my own creativity to bring him and the mysterious occupant of the confessional back once more into your hands.

The story nests between the past and the present. As is often the case with me, I had the ending secured and fixed first. The narrator's final destination in the closing scene is left entirely up to you. I have written a number of epilogues, and discarded them all. The story hinges on the uncertainty of what will happen, like the markets. The ending has an element of free will, and I only hope the narrator of the story went with his 'gut'.

FAMILIAR'S END

The tale was the first ever short story I completed, though not the first thing I actually wrote; that remains firmly locked in an impenetrable casket at the bottom of the sea. Heavily edited and changed from the original, it began life only as the central tale of the witch and familiar. It has an adventurous pacing that makes it a popular tale amongst my readers. The idea of dealing with the sins of the past by those who fate has determined is a theme that resonated with me. Doing a perfect stranger a good turn is one thing, but putting your life at risk helping someone with a four-hundred year old family problem is something else. If I ever build a house, then I will call it Familiar's End. The church at Croome Park, Worcestershire, is perched high above the vale and was likely in my thoughts. Cirencester Park may be the inspiration for the avenue; the trees are particularly dense on either side near the rise...

THE BOX IN THE BELFRY

I have visited many such belfries, having taken an interest in tower-ringing many years ago. I could ring a clashing touch of Cambridge, harsh enough to waken any spirit in the district, benign or otherwise. I always wondered what could be contained in those orbs that weathercocks sit upon.

It started life as a ghost tale but morphed into something more poignant. The idea of removing something from the world through accident and ignorance, only realising later its beneficial effects. It has an 'environmental' message, and a sense of not truly knowing something until it's gone.

The creature was inspired by the weathercock '*The Wherwell Cockatrice*', now in Andover Museum, that once adorned the steeple of St Peter and Holy Cross at Wherwell. The witches' circles can be seen on the hearths at the Fleece Inn, Bretforton, Worcestershire, a fifteenth-century thatched pub owned by the National Trust.

THE LAST LAUGH

Punch and Judy shows have always terrified me, but the men behind the striped canvas have intrigued me. This may stem from my early childhood remembrances of Cole Hawlings, the professor in John Masefield's *The Box of Delights*, and it signals Christmas in my mind whenever I hear the incidental music of the *Carol Symphony* by Victor Hely-Hutchinson.

I liked the idea of puppets taking on a life of their own, and committing vengeful and retaliatory murder against the thoroughly detestable Mr Galton, all against the pleasant sleepy summer backdrop of an English seaside town.

The final alliteration, '...*free from the sound of the swazzle, silent in all but the seabirds and the slumbering shore,*' was the genesis of the tale, but I have been told that it is almost impossible to pronounce while wearing the swazzle.

BELOVED

I have always been fascinated by immortality, and the drawbacks that living forever presents. From the simplest notions of being bored with food, once you'd tasted everything, to the grief of losing those mortal companions around you. Then there is the problem of people noticing you don't age...

Beloved is a companion and origin tale to *Thursday's Child*, which you can read for free as part of the sign up for my reader's group. It is the finale in my short story collection *Free Spirits*, and tells the story of the last surviving (or not!) child, saved and transformed by the magic of Sperrow Wood. *Beloved* was inspired by the image below:

Lundi looked out proudly and eternally from a great oil painting in a faraway gallery...

Woman with Cat | oil painting | Marguerite Gerard

TWO LEFT FEET

An unashamedly romantic ghost story about letting go, written in response to a digital image. It is not attributed but I would like to thank the creative for sparking the story into life. It is a story of resolving grief for both people, and draws heavily on a favourite film of mine, *Truly, Madly, Deeply*.

Printed in Great Britain
by Amazon

72329896R10137